WHEN FISHES FLEW

Wher

Josephine Poole

Fishes Flew

A Selection of Legends
and Old Wives' Tales
from the West Country

Illustrated by Barbara Swiderska

ERNEST BENN LIMITED
London & Tonbridge

First published 1978 by Ernest Benn Limited
25 New Street Square, London EC4A 3JA
& Sovereign Way, Tonbridge, Kent TN9 1RW

© Josephine Poole 1978
Illustrations © Ernest Benn Ltd. 1978

Printed in Great Britain
ISBN 0 510 15503-0

When fishes flew and forests walked
And figs grew upon thorn

G. K. Chesterton

Contents

I couldn't have written this book without help from many sources, for which I am most grateful. I would particularly like to thank Mr. Moss, Vicar of Cannington; Mr. Yates, Vicar of Haselbury Plucknett; and Mr. Robin Bush, Assistant Editor of the Victoria History of Somerset. The Taunton Public Library is an old friend, the staff are always obliging, and generous with their time and patience.

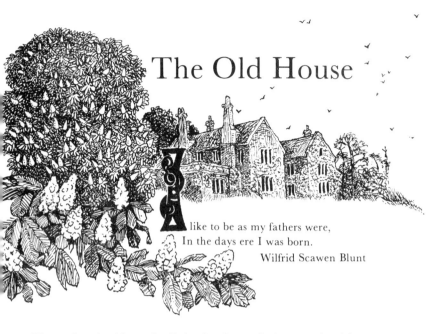

The Old House

like to be as my fathers were,
In the days ere I was born.

Wilfrid Scawen Blunt

Pippenhay had been built in the days of wings and gables, wine cellars and chimney stacks; there was a Tudor rose carved like a signature over the front door. It was made of uneven blocks of honey-coloured stone, and roofed with little slates that had aged to a tender grey. You could easily imagine faces peering from the heavy mullioned windows, through the panes which were too small to reflect more than a pocket handkerchief of garden or sky.

The house had the accumulated darkness that belongs to very old things, buildings or furniture or clothes or pictures or letters: a darkness of times and people gone for ever. It looked most homely in the evening, when its westerly walls and chimneys glowed in the sun dipping behind the trees, and every pane of glass on that side had a little bonfire in it.

The jackdaws called for "Jack – Jack!" all summer, and the sparrows hopped up and down the roofs, and cleaned their feathers in the weedy court that had been trodden, once upon a time, by the smartest carriage horses in the county. The starlings knew which chimneys were never used, and nested there; while swallows came every year to build under the beams in what had been the servants' hall, darting in and out through a broken window.

No servants now, of course: only one old lady left who looked after herself. Her use of the house had shrunk to those rooms small enough to heat, whose windows were not broken and whose ceilings didn't leak. The birds and the mice were encroaching. Her prayers got muddled with the voices of the rooks at twilight; in bed she could hear the mice skittering under the rafters or behind the panelling, they were company if she woke in the night.

"*Infested!*" said Alice Dory, when her husband inherited the house and they moved from London to live there. "I smelt mouse as soon as I came in. And the racket at night! And the feeling of being watched! *Horrible!*"

"I see you have a cat," said the old lady, Aunt Millicent, upright as a judge among the family slumped comfortably round the tea table. "I have lived here all my life, and never kept a cat." She stared contemptuously at Pounce, crouched glumly against the stove. He preferred London. "I like the birds," she said.

"Pounce never touches birds," said Alice firmly. "Only mice."

"Stop kicking your chair, Vincent," said Giles Dory. "Charlotte, take your elbows off the table." He was reading about root crops; he raised his head long enough to give these orders, then turned to the book again. Charlotte the eldest did as she was told. Vincent was ten, the sort of little bony boy who is never still. It was agony to

him to sit through a meal. As soon as his father's attention
was distracted, he went on hacking the chair.

Alice was expecting a baby. "I hope you won't find the
children too much, Aunt Mil," she said. "These two are
bad enough, and then there's the baby coming."

"Your children aren't noisy," said the old lady, with a
touch of scorn. "Now when my brothers and I were small,
we were always up to something. Noise!" She gave a thin
laugh. "We made the rafters ring!"

Giles left the table. He had never farmed before, and
he was enthusiastic. He was going to plant fodder turnips,
and buy some heifers next autumn.

The old Aunt had a way of drumming her bony fingers
on the table.

"As for Charlotte," she said, "I've hardly heard her
open her mouth. She's like a little ghost."

Charlotte blushed scarlet. Had she raised her eyes she
would have seen that her Great Aunt's expression was not
unkind. But she stared furiously at her plate.

"You can get down, Charlotte," said Alice kindly.
"Go in the garden, both of you; don't waste what's left of
the lovely day!"

They ran down the stone passage between the kitchen
and the hall. Vincent had a purpose, and ran faster.
"Where are you going?" Charlotte called, as he pulled
open the heavy front door. He didn't answer. The
afternoon sun streamed in. The door which was controlled
by a spring closed slowly, softly behind him, squeezing
out the sunlight after he had disappeared: even Vincent
couldn't slam that door.

Charlotte was left behind, feeling cross. At home – she
still meant London – she had had friends; there was the
park, the swimming pool, the library. She stared at their

old dining-room carpet, which her mother had laid in the middle of the hall floor. It looked like a raft in an ocean. She was surrounded by portraits of her ancestors: ramrod men in wigs and velvet, ladies with tiny waists in low-cut dresses, with picture hats and lap dogs. The mirror caught her, a thin dark girl, trapped like a changeling among these other Dorys. She turned her back on it and slipped through a door into the disused part of the house.

She found herself in a red and white paved hall, at the foot of a grand staircase. Above the landing a single window, much overgrown with virginia creeper, let in a cool green light. Some of the panes had gone, though, for little heaps of dead leaves had drifted into the corners. She started to climb the stairs. They were not so grand as they looked; the treads creaked, and were broken in places. Her fingers left a trail up the dusty mahogany banister. Even the cobwebs looked to let, and there were dead butterflies on the landing. But the creeper pressing the windowpanes was luminous, as if it too had been made out of glass.

When she reached the top, she went through an open door into an enormous room, that seemed almost as high as it was long. Its ceiling was arched like a tent, and moulded with Tudor roses and fleurs de lys. Over the huge stone fireplace there was more plaster decoration: two Indians armed with spears and quivers of arrows flanked a little scene where the sun shone diagonally upon a castle, and a woman knelt, holding a sheaf of corn. The windows were unshuttered, and these panes too were creepery, so that it was all bathed in soft, greeny rosy light.

Charlotte stood in the middle of the floor, and stretched her hand to her handsome invisible partner. With the other she displayed an imaginary crinoline, and very gravely danced her idea of a minuet. She danced in the light of a thousand candles, among fine company dressed as she was in waisted satin, keeping time to fiddles and drums. And there wasn't anybody, not anybody in the world she could have borne to see this dancing.

She ended with a deep curtsey. When she stood up again she was nineteen seventy seven Charlotte in a tee shirt and jeans, and going to the window she looked over the heap of garden rubbish that was going to be a bonfire when somebody had time, to the track that led down to the ford. Her father then appeared between the trees across the stream, trundling in his new secondhand tractor across the field called Big Mead with Vincent bumping behind in the trailer. The hedges were greening, and flowery with blackthorn, and beyond rose the wooded hills, bluey in the distance and sloping gently to the west, with the Wellington Monument like a finger pointing upward.

As she turned back into the room Charlotte noticed something lying in the corner of the windowsill. She picked it up. It was a very old, very dirty toy soldier. He wore a busby, and shouldered a gun, and weighed surprisingly heavy between her fingers, for he was made of lead.

He was only a fragment of somebody's past; but the shadow of that unknown somebody invested him with power. Holding him gave her a queer feeling, as if her shoes suddenly fitted into old footprints. She turned sharply from the window half-expecting to catch that somebody sneaking up behind her. She listened to her own steps walking firmly back to the landing. They were slower than her beating heart.

All round the landing there were doors she had not yet opened, but she felt she had done enough exploring.

She turned to the nearest, on the right. She rather prided herself on her sense of direction, and by her calculations this door ought to open into the upstairs passage in their own part of the house.

But it didn't.

It opened into a garret, and there was an old crone, and a spinning wheel.

Charlotte caught her breath.

The Duddlestones

An honest man, close-button'd to the chin,
Broad-cloth without, and a warm heart within.

William Cowper

Next instant she saw that the spinning wheel was really a sewing machine, the old-fashioned sort with a treadle; and then the crone turned her head and she recognised Aunt Mil. She was so relieved, her startled breath came out in quite a loud "Oh!".

Aunt Millicent was sewing a length of flowery curtain. It was marvellous material, scarlet and blue and green on gold, and as her needle flew in and out and she plucked together the piece she was darning, it shimmered as if it had a watery surface.

"I wondered which of you would find me first," she said, bending to her work again.

Charlotte was still clutching the little soldier. Now she walked forward and stood him on the table. Aunt Mil glanced at · him, without interrupting a stitch.

"That must have belonged to my brother Giles," she said. "He collected lead soldiers. Harry couldn't be bothered with them, it was all Navy with Harry. He was drowned, you know, in the First War."

"Your brother Giles was my grandfather," said Charlotte.

"That's right," said Aunt Mil, nodding without looking up. She clipped off the thread and unwound more, flicked it through the needle and went on again; her knotted old fingers moved quick as mice, and the shining curtain shimmered its fairy colours.

Charlotte went to the window. The sill was deep enough to sit on; she climbed up and wedged herself comfortably across its width, with her hands linked round her knees. She was high up, right at the top of the house. The rooks were considering settling for the evening: they were still flying, but in a preoccupied sort of way. A sweet smell like incense drifted in, from a poplar tree close by.

"Why Pippenhay?" she asked.

"Pippa was a Saxon chief," said Aunt Mil. "Hay was hay then as it is now, I suppose."

"What about Dory? Was he a chief, as well?"

"Oh no; the Dorys came from Normandy. Doré it would have been, meaning golden or gilded; I suppose we were rich in those days."

"Do you mean we came from Normandy with William the Conqueror? Did we fight at the Battle of Hastings?"

"I don't know," said Aunt Mil. "History does not relate. And if we did, is it anything to be proud of, when you consider that the flower of English chivalry was cut down that day, and died on the battlefield?"

"I didn't know there was English chivalry then," said Charlotte.

"Of course!" Aunt Mil sounded quite shocked. "The

Conquest was a disaster from many points of view, a return to the Dark Ages."

"But when did the Dorys come to Pippenhay?" asked Charlotte, after a silence.

"Early in the last century, when John Dory married Alicia Duddlestone. I expect you know all about the Duddlestones; your father must have told you."

"No."

"What, not told you about the Duddlestones? Oh, it's a nice story." Aunt Mil put down her sewing and looked across at Charlotte. "Let me see. What year was it, now, when Queen Anne came to the throne?"

Charlotte wasn't much good at dates, but her class happened to be doing Anne, so she said: "Seventeen hundred and two, I think."

"That's right." Aunt Mil took up her work again and began to sew more quickly than ever; the light was going, and she wanted to finish the darn. "Well, that year she made a Western Progress. You know what that is – a slow journey from great house to great house, and very expensive for the lords and ladies who had to offer hospitality. There were loyal addresses and tableaux, and exhibitions of rural art and folk dancing; and no doubt it poured with rain, just as it does now whenever there is a gymkhana or a flower show.

"The Queen made this Western Progress partly for her husband's sake, because he suffered from asthma; I suppose she thought the country air would do him good. He was Prince George from Denmark, as no doubt you remember; a friendly, good-humoured sort of person. He was naturally interested in the English way of life, and while they were staying near Bristol, he decided to spend an hour or two at the Exchange. So off he set, with just one officer for guard and company."

"What was the Exchange?" asked Charlotte.

"That was where they bought and sold corn in those days, and a very lively scene it was. The Prince stayed there longer than he meant, looking and listening, until all the merchants had gone. Of course none of them would have dreamt of inviting him back to lunch, or anything of that sort.

But Prince George had noticed a comical sort of fellow, who had been sucking the knob of his stick and staring at him most of the morning; and now this individual plucked up his courage and off with his hat, and coming up to the Prince bluntly introduced himself. "John Duddlestone of Corn Street," he said, "and very much at your service, though only a humble bodice maker; but are you, Sir, the husband of our good Queen Anne, as folks do say you are?"

The Prince was rather surprised, but agreed that this was so.

"It bothered me to see none of the prime merchants on 'Change 've invited ye home. Believe me," insisted the honest man, rubbing his fingers through his hair so that it stood up on end, "'tis no lack of love or loyalty on their parts; they'm just shy to presume with so great a man. Still what shame to our city, if the husband of our Queen were forced to dine at an inn, for that none had invited him! So to be short, and to make all right: allow me, Sir, to beg you – humble and unworthy that I am – to come home with me to dinner. 'Tis but a step, and bring your soldier officer along with ye; that is if ye can eat what we have to offer, a good piece of roast beef and plum pudding, and as much ale as ye've a mind to, brewed by my wife, and as good as any in the city!"

Prince George nearly burst out laughing at this original invitation. However he accepted it with a polite little speech, though in fact dinner had already been ordered for him at the White Lion. So he walked off to Corn Street with his officer and the loyal bodice maker, and when they arrived at his house, John Duddlestone ushered them in.

"Wife!" he bawled from the foot of the stairs. "Wife! Put on a clean apron and come down, for the Queen's husband and a soldier gentleman are come to dine with us!"

Dame Duddlestone hurried down at once in a clean blue apron, and she looked so homely and friendly and good-hearted that Prince George couldn't help kissing her as soon as she came into the parlour.

Conversation was a little tricky at first during dinner, before the ale had really begun to flow. The Prince behaved with his most careful company manners.

He asked his host if he ever went to London. "Oh, aye," John replied with his mouth full. "Now and then; now the ladies 've chosen to wear stays 'stead of bodices, sometimes I go thither to buy whalebone."

Goodness knows how the officer managed to get through that dinner with a straight face; I hope the Prince made him a general! But Prince George was touched as well as amused by Duddlestone's kindness. He knew that anything in the house was his for the asking, humble though it was; and he was anxious to repay such hospitality. So when he left, full of beef and pudding and first-rate ale, he made a bargain with the bodice maker. He made him promise to bring his wife with him, next time he visited London, and he gave him a card which he said would admit them both to Windsor Castle.

So when John Duddlestone went to London again for another supply of whalebone, his dame rode pillion behind him. And when their business was done they kept their promise, and went on to Windsor Castle. Sure enough, the card was like a magic key: the Duddlestones were shown in, and passed from one gorgeous footman to another, until they arrived at Prince George himself. He was very pleased to see them again, and presented them to the Queen.

Her Majesty looked at them, and smiled, and held out her hands. You couldn't stand on ceremony with the Duddlestones, they were such natural folk. She thanked them for looking after her husband, and said that now it was her turn to ask them to dine. Of course they had nothing suitable to wear, but Her Majesty wouldn't hear of that excuse. She told them she wanted to give them a present of Court dress for the occasion; she would provide everything, only they must choose the material. Mr. and Mrs. Duddlestone hardly knew what to say as they looked about them; even the curtains there were made of grander stuff than anything they owned. But at last they decided on purple velvet, as it was what Prince George was wearing at the time.

So the royal dressmakers were summoned with their tape measures, and the splendid clothes were ready in time for dinner. Then indeed John Duddlestone looked as prime as any of the merchants on 'Change! As for his wife – he thought her the finest in all the company, saving the Queen; and when he heard them both being introduced as "the most loyal persons in the City of Bristol", he thought he would burst with pride.

But his glory was not yet over, for after dinner the Queen ordered him to kneel; and as Mrs. Duddlestone never tired of relating after, she first laid a sword on his head, and then said: "Stand up, Sir John!" . . ."

The window where Charlotte was sitting had a fiery frame, but darkness was inching from the corners of the garret room. Aunt Millicent's darn was finished. She put away her needle and thread. The beautiful curtain lay like a Court dress over her knees.

"What happened then?" Charlotte spoke very softly.

"Queen Anne offered Sir John Duddlestone a place in the government, or a present of money; but he turned it down. "We want for nothing," he said. "We've fifty pounds of savings put by; and mind you," he added with a wink, rubbing his nose to show her that he wasn't born yesterday, "from the number of folks I see about Your Majesty's house, I doubt not your living must cost very dear!"

Then the Queen with a smile took Lady Duddlestone's hand, and unfastening her own gold watch from her belt, made her accept it. Well! That watch was a treasure the good woman valued above everything for the rest of her life! She always wore it over her blue apron, when she went to Bristol market."

*　　*　　*

"Come and see where the kestrels are nesting," said Giles that evening, when everyone met in the kitchen for supper.

Alice moved the scrambled egg pan to the cool side of the stove, and they all walked down the field in front of the house. A huge oak grew at the bottom, near the stream. They stood underneath and looked up. High in the trunk there was a hole, with tell-tale splatters of white on the branches below it.

"They used to nest here when I was a boy. You'll hear the young squealing like piglets in a week or two," said Giles happily.

The country had turned the sombre colours left in a worn-out paintbox; and as if they had run a little, a misty darkness was spreading behind the trees. But far overhead where the sky was still clear, a jet caught the now invisible sun. Burnished to copper it mounted its wide arc, trailing glorious streamers; while its noise, despairing of the climb, came much later, and seemed to belong to quite a different machine.

They walked back to the house.

The Fairies

Up the airy mountain, down the rushy glen,
We daren't go a-hunting for fear of little men.
William Allingham

It was half-term, and the sort of spring morning when the sun shines its brightest, the birds sing their sweetest, and you can almost hear the grass grow. Charlotte and Vincent were enjoying the luxury of a long-drawn-out family breakfast. Vincent was looking particularly holy, with his grazed knees hidden under the table, and his hair smarmed with a wet brush. He was quietly consuming toast. It was his eighth piece.

The family calm was shattered by Aunt Mil, who exclaimed with sudden passion: "*Must* that child *finish* the marmalade?"

"Stop it, Vincent!" said Giles, startled from the 'Somerset Farmer'. "You've had enough."

"Love," said Alice, looking up from a letter she had been reading, "you know the Oatens are coming in to do the larder wall? While they're at it, couldn't they give the room next to Vincent's a coat of paint? It would be cheaper than having them in specially, and all our friends seem determined to come and stay!"

Giles wanted to read about the pros and cons of three cuts of silage; he grunted in what he hoped was a non-committal way.

The Oatens turned up that morning, father and son – the same family had worked at Pippenhay for generations. Son was slim, with glasses and receding, straw-coloured hair; there was something dapper, even dashing about him. His working jersey and trousers were old, but he wore an exciting tie. His father had twinkling eyes and wore a cap; his trousers had bags where his knees fitted.

The larder wall needed plastering, which meant moving the huge old fridge. That was when disaster struck: creak, groan, and it lurched through the floor in a drunken stagger. The Oatens stood and stared at it, and scratched their heads. Then young Oaten went off to look for Giles, while old Oaten balanced the fridge in his arms, and Vincent jumped up and down at the other end of the larder. But he wasn't heavy enough to go through the floor.

Aunt Millicent passed along the passage and said: "Ha, Mr. Oaten, good morning. How is Mrs. Oaten?" And old Oaten touched his cap and smiled, and said: "Very well, Ma'am, thankee, considerin'." Then Giles and young Oaten came back and they had a consultation, and jumped experimentally and burst several more boards; when it was decided that the whole floor would have to be re-newed.

So that was how Alice got her spare room, even sooner than she hoped. While young Oaten went away to order chipboard for the larder, old Oaten moved upstairs to start soaking off wallpaper. He took his cap off when he worked indoors, as if he was in church, and tied a huge white apron round himself.

Vincent fetched another brush and helped. When it was lunch, he carried bread and cheese and an apple up to the spare room, to eat with Oaten. Oaten sat on the up-turned bucket, Vincent on the steps. They were companionable without talking much. Oaten had a plastic box of sandwiches, and strong tea in a flask. His shirt was open to the third button; the neck of his vest showed. His chest and arm fur was paler than his skin.

It was a very hot day. The window overlooked the wing of the house where the servants had lived; there were licheny slates lying loose on the roof, and a swallow darted in and out through a broken pane, where there was a fern growing on the wrong side of the glass.

"D'you think there's ghosts here?" Vincent asked. This question had been exercising his mind since they moved in, and he reckoned old Oaten (unlike the other grown-ups in the house) would tell him.

"Never heard so. Never seen nothing."

"It's awfully old. Haven't you ever found any old bones, or bloodstains, or anything?"

Oaten shook his head. He pulled an old baccy tin out of his pocket and began rolling himself a cigarette. Vincent watched his fingers, thick and red they were, but very neat with the wispy paper and tobacco.

"Heard tell o' the fairies," Oaten suggested, as a possible substitute.

"*Fairies!*" expostulated Vincent, with infinite scorn.

"'Twere a long time ago, mind," Oaten excused the story. He licked along the edge of the paper. Very gently he kept rolling the cigarette into shape, while he waited for the lick to dry.

"What about the fairies?" Perhaps they were better than nothing.

"Ah! Never seen 'em myself, mind; don't know anybody as has; this is going back I don't know how long. Right back to the olden days; you'll know more about them days nor me; never did have much headucation."

Vincent nodded in a superior way from the top of the steps.

"If you want to know about them fairies, you got to think of Taunton like it was then. 'Twas all dirt roads in them days, so there'd 've been plenty of mud three-quarters of the year. Boats come up the river to the Tone Bridge, and every inn had a green bough hanging over, to let you know they sold liquor."

Old Oaten put the cigarette between his lips, struck a match, and lit it; the spent match he tossed accurately out of the window.

"There was the Garlic Fair, which folks did say made 'em strong-winded; 'spect it did too. The garlic come from Bridgwater by boat. Then there was the Horse Fair – don't know how well you know Taunton, but 'twas up towards the Staplegrove Road. On fair days the cattle and sheep stood all along of Bridge Street and up North Street, mooing and maaing all through the town. Then there was the donkey racing, and folks jumping along in sacks, and blindfold wheelbarrow racing along a road with a great open ditch to one side of it, you can guess they often toppled into that, and how everybody laughed!"

Old Oaten's country voice, and the spellbound spring afternoon, made it seem very real.

"Then the women would run races for smocks – not just the young ones, neither. There was gingerbread stalls, and fruit to eat, and they was biting hot rolls and treacle hanging on a string – something like apple bobbing today. And the young fellows would climb up the greasy pole, to try and win a leg of mutton. They had the greasy pole opposite.the Kings Arms, at the bottom of the Staplegrove Road. There was wrestling, and dancing.

I seen barbecues advertised, and dancing till all hours in a field, but 'tisn't the same I don't suppose. Folks don't live no more like they used to."

His cigarette finished, he got up and carried the bucket he had been sitting on, into the bathroom next door to fill it with water. Vincent stayed where he was, on the steps. Oaten came back and dipping his big brush, went on sploshing the wall. All his actions were slow and considered. He grubbed up a loose corner: off it peeled like buttered paper.

"Tell about the fairies."

"Ah, them fairies! Hadn't got on to that, had I?" He paused, as if he doubted whether it was worth telling. Vincent waited.

"His name was Jeremiah Thatcher, but 'tis no good your asking me how long ago, for I can't give you no answer.

He lived at Combe St. Nicholas, that's up over the hill in the Chard direction. 'Tween Corfe and Chard. I suppose his family had been thatchers once, but Jeremiah was a farmer. Used to come down to Taunton every month if the weather was right, to market. They had the market once a month in those days, not every week like it is now.

Times Jem hadn't got nothing to buy and sell, still 'twas a chance to meet his friends, find out who had got the hay in, and what the weather was doing all round. Plenty of green boughs hanging out along the street on a market day; so he'd turn in under one of them, and get the dust out of his throat with good strong cider like they made it then, and shake his head over the price of corn.

He was always late starting off home, but that didn't matter; his wife'd get on with the milking if he wasn't back. The journey seemed shorter, see, the more he drank, and his horse seemed faster. Still at last he turned out his pockets and he hadn't no more money to drink, so he heaved himself up on his old black gelding and jogged off t'wards Corfe Hill.

Reckon you might've seen several such, leaving Taunton about this time of a market day, all slewed up with scrumpy, blobbing about first one way, then t'other, and lucky the horses knows their way home, for the farmers don't!"

Oaten paused, and worked at the wall for some minutes before he spoke again; but in imagination he was far away, toiling up Corfe Hill giddy with cider, uncounted years ago.

"Jem kept his feet stuck firm in the stirrups, still he nearly come off each time he hit at the flies. 'Tis a long pull up that hill, even today: ten to one you'll get stuck behind a lorry and have to crawl. They was working the stone-quarry then. 'Spect he heard the clink of the hammers on rock; maybe passed a horse and cart. And they was charcoal burning in the woods: the smoke of the fires showed up feathery blue between the trees. Smells of autumn, woodsmoke, I always think – short days, and long pleasant evenings. Didn't make him feel no cooler.

There'd 've been beeches then like there is today, casting shade along the track; but there wouldn't 've been no fields along the top. 'Twould 've been a heathery, scrubby sort of country in those days. You'd still 've seen right across the Vale to the Quantocks and the Bristol

Channel – Wales too, on a clear day. Jem's head ached fit to crack if he looked any further than his horse's ears. Now and then he'd wipe at his face, but it took him as long to get out his handkerchief, as it did to find a pocket to put it in, so he might as well not 've bothered. And the sun 'd soon be down; he'd be lucky to get home before nightfall. "Drat 'e!" he swore at the sun. "Drat 'e!" says he to the flies mistaking his bald patch for a skating rink; swipes at 'em with his hat, and nearly falls off again.

All of a sudden the old horse stopped dead, without any warning at all. Over Jem went, plump into the ditch, which was fortunately dry and full of dead leaves. He lied there a minute, with all the breath knocked out of him.

What's up with the animal, anyways? Never acted like that before.

There he is, cropping the grass along the track as if nothing 'd happened. Jem staggered up to him and give him a kick before he hauled himself on again.

They got round the next bend in the track, and the horse stopped again. This time Jem didn't fall off. But he sat there rubbing his eyes as if he was dreaming. For in front of him, spread over the hill on both sides of the track, was a great company of little people, just like country folks at a fair. Enough to make a man stare and scratch his head! Why, there's tinkers, and cobblers; pedlars with trays of ribbons and trinkets of all sorts; stands of fruit and drinking booths. The tallest of 'em's no bigger nor a small man, and their clothes 's very bright – little cloaks and gowns and breeches of blue and red and green; and they'd high crowns to their hats. They was all bustling about and chattering in some furrin lingo; he couldn't understand a word.

So Jem wondered where they was off to; maybe the
fair at Churchinford; but then thinking it over, it couldn't
be that, for 'twasn't the season. Then he started
grinning, and shaking his head, for he was remembering
tales he'd heard of the fairies that side of the hill. Didn't
believe it, of course. Didn't believe it even now when there
he sat looking at them.

He was thirsty, though. It's thirsty work, Corfe Hill is,
and the more he looked at the drinks laid out in the little
booths, the more he thought he'd like to try them. So he
kicked up his horse, meaning to ride in among the little
people.

The horse 'd got more sense than Jeremiah Thatcher,
and he didn't want to move. Still old Jem went on, kick
kick kick, and swiped at him with his hat; so at last
the faithful beast give his head a shake, as if to say:
"You'll regret it," and in he went.

Now I guess Jem imagined them fairies to be some sort
of scrumpy dream, that 'd vanish so soon as he got up to
them; and that was what did happen in a way. Little
folks, and goods and stands, drinks and everything – it
all just melted into thin air as he rode in, there was
nought to be seen but gorse and bracken and the silvery
trunks of the trees. But old Jem had all the time the
horrible feeling of being butted and jostled, as if they still
crowded all round him. And then his old horse what he'd
reared himself and known all his life, and was lucky if
he got given a bucket of oats in a year – he was trembling
and sweating like a thoroughbred. Still Jem pushed on a
little distance, being an obstinate old beggar that didn't
like to be made a monkey of; and then he stopped and
looked back. Bless me, if there wasn't the fair, just as it had
been, laid out on the hill behind him!

But he didn't get the chance to look at it for long, for his horse took hold of the bit and bolted him home as if all the devils in hell was after him. Jem was bumped and banged to bits by the time he reached his farm; he pretty well fell out of the saddle. And he didn't get much sympathy from his wife. He tried to tell her what happened, but she reckoned worse dreams nor that come out of a bottle!

Next day he was so terrible lame, he could hardly crawl out of bed. You could count the bruises all down one side, and they lasted the rest of his life. So he give over the farm to his wife and sons, and on fine days he'd sit out in his chair, out in the front, and folks would come from far and wide to hear him tell what happened. If they brought a bottle of cider with them, so much the better – they'd get more of a three-dimensional version of the story. He lived on for another twenty year, with his nose getting redder and his side stiffer, until he could hardly hobble. But if anyone said it might 've been sunstroke he'd had, or a mug or so too much cider, he was very energetic in arguing the point. There was never a man so convinced of the fairies as Jeremiah Thatcher!"

"I should think it must have been the cider," said Vincent.

"Tanglefoot, we call it. Tangle your feet up, and tumble you down on your nose. P'raps 'twas. For all that, if ever I see such a fair-keeping on the hill, I shan't venture in among them. Reckon everyone that has, has got great damage by it."

Oaten peeled off a swath of wallpaper as he spoke, exposing the wall's inmost skin. It was very, very old, and stuck so tight, old Oaten reached for his scraper.

"How are you getting on?" said Alice, coming in at that moment. "What a frightful job!" She moved between

Oaten and Vincent. "What's this one you're getting off now?"

"'Tis the devil to shift, ma'am. Must've been up I don't know how long."

"Let me see." Alice, who was rather short-sighted, peered closely at the wall. When she turned round she looked excited.

"It must be one of the very first nursery wallpapers!" she said. "If you look carefully you can see part of the old design; I think it's John Gilpin, by Caldecott. Aunt Mil said this room was used as a nursery when she was a child."

The Oatens managed to save a whole width of the Caldecott paper. They soaked pieces clean in the bath to patch its holes, and varnished it with loving care. Each little scene had a frame of leaves and flowers. There were the loving Gilpins at breakfast, with baby in his high-chair. Next came the fond farewell, with the ladies busted like figureheads; then the unfortunate citizen was dashing away in mid-bolt, in a flurry of geese and dogs, with his head blown bald as a quince. Aunt Mil was moved to see it again, with its innocent memories of her brothers Giles and Harry.

Fair Rosamund

IS banner over me was love.
The Song of Solomon

The apple trees were in blossom. Every garden had its show of pink and white; while at Pippenhay they flowered in acres, for Giles was growing apples simply because the trees were already there in two rough little orchards. They hadn't been pruned for years, and twisted and bent in every direction. He hoped to sell this year's crop for cider, and he wanted advice on how to make the most of it.

He was told to spray, he was told that it was too late in the year; he was told to fertilise, he was told that if he did he would get all leaf and no apples. He became confused. Finally he heard that the Farm Institute at Cannington was having an Open Day, so he decided to go along and pick their brains; and because it was Saturday, he took Charlotte and Vincent with him.

It was a beautifully fine, windy day, with patches of cloud scudding across the sky and drawing enormous shadows over the sloping fields. The banks along the lanes were full of campions and stitchwort and wild strawberry flowers. Giles was a bad driver, especially when he was preoccupied, and they had several exciting close shaves. Farm tractors were the worst hazard, with a way of looming unexpectedly round corners.

They stopped at a village shop and bought ice-creams. A curlew cried, long and long, as they approached the sea, and the fields got flatter. "Bridgwater, six miles," Charlotte read aloud as they stopped at a road junction.

"Admiral Blake," said Giles. "He was born there, in the house which is now the Blake Museum. All clear your side, Charly?"

"There's a coach coming," she said doubtfully.

"My dear girl, we've got masses of time. Masses," he said, swinging the car adroitly in front of the cursing bus, and speeding down the road. "Next left I think. Why hoot, you miserable man?"

"You should've indicated," said Vincent.

"Don't back-seat drive."

Cannington was full of people and cars.

"I think you're meant to park over there," said Charlotte, pointing to an official in armbands directing the traffic.

"Why tell him? He won't take any notice," came Vincent's bored voice from the back.

He was right. Giles whisked down a side street and drew up against a house whose windows had net curtains primly drawn. They all got out, and locked the car.

The apple orchards were on the far side of the village. Crowds of people seemed to be going in that direction.

"Why don't you two wait for me somewhere?" said Giles, as they were hustled and shoved from all sides. "Here, you can get yourselves more ice-cream," he gave them some change. "Where shall we meet? I know, the church," noticing its red tower standing high over the roofs, with its gilt clock and cockalorum weather vane. "I'll pick you up there as quick as I can, but I don't expect it'll be under an hour." He raised his hand, and soon disappeared in the crowd.

Charlotte and Vincent turned between the old houses in the direction of the church. It was quiet, and very hot. Swallows were swooping and darting overhead, as they had every summer for hundreds upon hundreds of years.

"Nice," said Charlotte.

"I wanted to see the farm machinery."

"Go on then. It'll be in that modern block we passed on the way in, you remember. Anyhow there's a notice at the drive end. I'll wait for you here," she said, going into the churchyard. "I'll be sitting under those trees over there. And look, you take the money, and get the ice-cream on your way back."

"Okay. I won't be long."

"Watch it across the road."

"Okay."

He pocketed the change and ran off.

"Get some crisps as well if you can," she called after him. He waved to show he had heard her, without turning round.

Charlotte went into the church. It was cool, and deeply still. When her eyes adjusted to the light she noticed the beautiful little painted angels holding shields under the beams in the side aisles, and the carved bosses in the ceiling. Hidden among these at one end was a face like a pig's, squinting and blowing a raspberry.

She walked up the aisle and came to a wooden statue of a girl about her own age. Beside it a slab in the floor said: 'The Child of Cannington. The name is known to God.' She was looking at this when she realised that someone had come up behind her, and she turned quickly.

"Sorry," said the stranger, with a smile. "I'm always told I go about like a thief in the night, but I didn't mean to scare you."

"Who was the Child?" asked Charlotte.

"Nobody knows. The bones were discovered about ten years ago when an old burial ground was being excavated near here. The Child must have been a local saint, because there was evidence that pilgrims visited the grave, in the times of the very first Christians."

He was a young man, with dark hair and eyes, and a quick, enthusiastic manner; he was wearing a suit with a white polo-necked tee shirt. It crossed Charlotte's mind that he might be the vicar, and at that moment he remarked: "I'm studying theology." He walked ahead of her into the chancel. "Not yet ordained, though that will be soon, I hope. I'm staying with very long-suffering aunts in the village. Please call me Simon," he said, turning to shake hands.

"I'm Charlotte."

"Now here's something that'll interest you," he went on, pointing to a wrought-iron screen in front of the organ. "That's from the tomb of one of the Cliffords – Lord Hugh; that's his coat of arms in the middle. Those things like serpents supporting the shield are called wyverns."

He paused, looking expectantly at Charlotte. "Doesn't the name Clifford mean anything to you?"

"No."

"But you must have heard of Fair Rosamund!"

"I don't think so."

"What! not: 'When that King Henry ruled this land, the

second of that name, besides the queen, he dearly loved a fair and comely dame – ' ?" He trumpeted the quotation in the quiet church.

"I'm afraid not."

"Rosamund Clifford," he said. "A Child of quite a different sort. Would you like me to tell you about her?"

"Yes," she said politely. She couldn't help smiling because he was so serious and so enthusiastic; but she was anxious not to hurt his feelings. "Yes, please."

"Then let's go outside and sit in the sun; there's nothing so penitential as a church pew." But he paused on the threshold.

"You see those gargoyles up there, over the porch? Sort of batlike creatures? Now don't you think they might be wyverns?"

Charlotte looked up at them, screwing her face against the sun. "Maybe. But the others had long noses, like dogs or wolves; these have snouts."

"They might have had noses once. The noses might have weathered away. Now, where shall we sit?"

She led the way to the trees she had noticed earlier, and they settled themselves comfortably beneath them. The churchyard was very neat, mown close, with carefully clipped yews. There were a few gravestones left, but the mounds had been levelled. The ancient sleepers had been ousted from their beds; it was a garden now, not a cemetery. Behind them was the vicarage, with a blue-painted door.

"There's a prayer you may remember, if you go to church, which says something about being 'godly and quietly governed'," Simon began, wedging his back against a tree, and clasping his hands round his knees. "Well, we are back in the days of Stephen and Matilda, and England wasn't. There was trouble in Scotland and Ireland and Wales, and expeditions had to be sent to try to sort things out, which was very difficult and expensive. Worst of all, the most powerful families in England couldn't agree. Seeds of discord were sown then, which finally bore bitter fruit in the Wars of the Roses."

Charlotte hoped inwardly that it wasn't going to be a history lesson.

"The Baron de Clifford was one of the fighting barons of the Welsh Marches. Clifford Castle, where he lived, is in Herefordshire; but his wife's mother was a Mohun and lived at Dunster – that's a few miles along the coast from here, on the Minehead road."

"*I* know", said Charlotte. "There's a castle, and a covered market where they used to sell wool. We spent a day there walking in the woods, it was lovely."

"That's right," he said, returning her with a wave of his hand to the twelfth century.

"Now the Cliffords spent a lot of time travelling about between their various castles and estates. They had a manor at Cannington, and it was here that Lady Margaret Clifford gave birth to a daughter, whom they called Joan. She was a delicate little thing, so it was decided to ask the nuns to look after her.

The nuns, the poor nuns! Look over there, beyond the church, and you will see pretty well all that is left of Cannington Priory. It had been founded by Baron de Courcy, of Stoke Courcy (or Stogursey as we know it); it consisted of about a dozen religious, and the children of the local gentry were sent to them to be educated. They were honoured to take in the baby daughter of such rich and influential people as the Cliffords – "

"Did they want her to grow up into a nun?" interrupted Charlotte.

"No, no, there was no agreement of that sort.

Joan was very pretty, and the older she grew, the lovelier she became; until she was so extraordinarily beautiful that nobody called her Joan any more. They called her Rose, the Rose of Cannington, the Rose of the West, the Rose of the World – Rosamund.

Whenever the Cliffords visited Cannington, they took Rosamund to live with them. They had quantities of friends, all rich and noble, powerful barons and fashionable ladies; even as a tiny child she must have noticed the difference between them, and the nuns. Of course everyone admired her tremendously (it was one way of keeping on the right side of her father), but she felt more at home in the convent. She was glad to go back to the little room she shared with Sister Cecilia, who was young and pretty, and played the lute. When their work was done they sat together at the window, and Rosamund got on with her embroidery while Sister Cecilia sang the latest French songs – in a low voice, so that the Prioress couldn't hear her.

Sister Cecilia had a spiritual relationship with Roland, son of Charlemagne; she had never met him as he had perished at Roncevalles hundreds of years before, but she knew a long poem about him, and when she recited it, it made her and Rosamund cry. Rosamund knew a French boy, who sometimes came to stay with her parents at Cannington, but she wasn't sure at first whether she liked him or not. He was called Henry of Anjou. The flattering part of it was that although he was as rough and bullying as her brothers, he always made a point of being nice to her. "He's in love with you," said Sister Cecilia when she told her about it. And Sister Cecilia sighed, and played a sad little tune on her lute.

Henry was an Important Person, although he was so young. Rosamund saw this, although she didn't understand why even her father's grandest friends treated him politely. As soon as he opened his mouth to speak there was a respectful silence: even when he answered back, or talked nonsense, or lost his temper. Her brothers envied him, though his clothes were often scruffy and he forgot to brush his hair; but Rosamund thought he looked lonely.

By and by she realised that when he came it was like spring, and when he went away it was winter. "You're in love with him," said Sister Cecilia, with a sigh for herself, and a smile for her friend.

Henry and Rosamund went fishing one summer afternoon. He couldn't catch anything, and lost his temper, and broke up the rods. So they climbed the sloping trunk of a willow and made a nest for themselves in the fork; and Henry forgot his grudge against the fish, and began to dream. His dreams were always on a magnificent scale.

"What would you do," he asked, picking at the bark of the tree, looking away to disguise the importance of the question, "if I were King of England?"

"I should be pleased," said the dutiful Rosamund.

"Yes, but imagine what you'd do. Wouldn't you kneel before me and kiss my ring, and swear to be my loyal subject so long as you shall live?"

"Of course I would!"

"And then, supposing I took your lilywhite hand and raised you up, and begged you – no, I would probably command you – to be my queen, Rosamund – what would you do then? What would you say?"

"I would thank you, I suppose."

Henry frowned; she was not entering properly into the spirit of the dream.

"But would you accept, and make me the happiest of princes; or turning your lovely face away, would you suffer yourself to be led into the deepest dungeon in the Tower, there to languish until you died a sacrifice upon the altar of unrequited love?"

"I don't understand," said Rosamund, and looked as if she was going to cry.

"It isn't very complicated: all the French poems are written in that sort of language; but I suppose your nuns only talk Latin. What order are they anyway, the country bumpkins?"

"Benedictines," Rosamund said stiffly. She had never told him about Sister Cecilia. She did not like him to sneer at the nuns.

There was a silence. When Henry spoke again he sounded more agreeable.

"I would be wearing sweeping red velvet, trimmed with ermine and lined with cloth of gold; and you would be robed in white samite – I'm not sure what that is, but something pretty special. I would let out your hair," he touched her plait as he spoke, "and it would fall in a rippling flood down your back, glittering more precious to me than gold, in the light of a million candles. We would be married and crowned all in one go and the Pope would do it; we would kneel reverently before him while the crowns, matching but mine would be bigger, were placed on our brows; and then we would turn and face the populace, and a mighty howl would go up – "Hail, Henry, King of England! Long life to Henry! God bless the King!" Doesn't that give you shivers down your spine?"

he asked, putting his arm round her and squeezing her enthusiastically.

"But I don't want to be a queen," said Rosamund, looking frightened.

"What a baby you are!" he said, nuzzling her cheek. "You know I'd look after you. You wouldn't want to stand in my way, would you?"

"Oh no," she said. She was sure of that. And as Henry still sat there entranced by his dreams, she thought of asking: "Why was your crown bigger than mine?"

"Because I've got a larger head," he lied at once."

Vincent flopped down between them, and Charlotte jumped. She had been so engrossed in the story, she hadn't heard him coming over the grass. He had an ice-cream in each hand, and packets of crisps bulged in his trousers pockets. They divided everything into three.

"Go on about Rosamund," said Charlotte.

Vincent wiped his mouth on his arm and licked off the surplus. "What're you talking about?"

"Fair Rosamund," Charlotte told him. "We've got up to where she and Henry have fallen in love."

Vincent gave a theatrical groan.

"Go back to your beastly old machinery if you don't want to listen. What was it like, anyway?"

"Smashing." But he had seen enough. He lay on his back with his arms linked under his head, and the ants and spiders explored him, but he didn't mind.

"So the Cliffords moved on from Cannington," Simon went on. "And with them went their friends and relations and cooks and scullions and grooms and guards, in a slow procession across country. Every few miles they had to stop to hear grievances, or receive messages from the Court, so it took ages to get back to Clifford Castle. Henry of

Anjou returned to his uncle and guardian, Robert Earl of Gloucester; and Rosamund went back to the priory and her dear nuns, and took up the embroidery she had left there. She liked sewing, sitting in a quiet place thinking peaceful thoughts, while her neat little fingers worked at an elaborate pattern.

Soon after this Henry lost his wise uncle. Now he had no permanent home, but was shuttled about between the castles and palaces. He grew up quickly. He was louder, more assured; he stopped trying to control his temper, but used it to get his own way; and though he was just as ambitious, he learnt to keep his dreams to himself.

When he was sixteen he went to Scotland, and King David made him a knight; and then he came back to Cannington.

Rosamund thought he was marvellous. And she was so beautiful, it took his breath away. He knew she was truthful and innocent, and her love had nothing selfish in it; alone among all the people, both men and women, who flattered him and fed his ambition, Rosamund loved him as freely as a child, without any idea of gaining anything by it. That was what made her precious to him; and that was why he betrayed her.

He told her he loved her, all the time, in the most fashionable language; but she could have read it anyway in his ardent face. She was not very good at expressing her own feelings, but she embroidered him a beautiful pair of gloves. Henry kept them inside his shirt, next to his heart. He visited the convent and gave presents to the nuns, nothing very handsome, because he was poor in those days; but all he could afford, to please Rosamund."

"I like him," said Charlotte softly.

"Well! You may not by the end of the story. But it must

have been very difficult for him, not knowing whether it was going to be ermine, or the Tower.

You can guess what happened next. The time came for Henry to leave, but still he lingered; and at last when he had to go, Rosamund went with him.

They weren't married, and of course Rosamund couldn't tell the nuns that she was running away with him; she simply went. But she did confide in Sister Cecilia, and before she left she gave her a ring, the only jewel she had that Henry hadn't given her. I can tell you exactly what it looked like: the stone was a sapphire, supported by four tiny wyverns with outspread wings, and it had 'Hail Mary full of grace' engraved round it, in Latin.

Sister Cecilia begged her to take her lute, but Rosamund wasn't musical, and couldn't play. So the faithful friends said good-bye, with kisses and tears, and in fact they never saw each other again.

Henry took Rosamund to Woodstock, which is near Oxford, and here their first son was born. They called him William. Alas! Very soon after his birth, Henry was summoned urgently to France. How passionately he swore he would be true to Rosamund! I wonder if she believed him.

Three years passed, and very dreary they might have been; but the nuns had taught Rosamund the virtues of patience and fortitude. The nice little baby was an interest, and there was always her embroidery. And she soon had friends about her; she was the kind of girl you couldn't help liking.

Meanwhile, how was Henry spending his time?

In 1151, a year after he left her, he became Earl of Anjou and Maine. And now the dreams were becoming realities, and ambition began to dominate love and honour.

For Eleanor of Aquitaine was obtaining a divorce from her husband, King Louis VII, and she was the sort of woman any prince might admire. She was not as beautiful as Rosamund, but she was very good-looking; she was worldly, intelligent, and dowered with the finest provinces in the South of France. Eleanor would never have consented to the rather inefficient secrecy of Woodstock Manor. Six weeks after she regained her freedom, in 1152, she married Henry. She was thirty-two; he was not yet twenty."

"Rotten egg," said Vincent.

"Remember the Tower," said Charlotte. "Think what it must have been like in those days. What did Rosamund do?"

"Threw a wobbler, I bet!"

"Henry came back the next year. He left Eleanor in Normandy – by that time she'd had a baby son, as well – and he borrowed her fleet, and sailed to England. King Stephen was forced to make him his heir. Henry stayed a year in his prospective kingdom, and he visited Woodstock. He sent a mutual friend ahead of him, to break the news of his marriage to Rosamund, but actually she knew already; news of that sort always travels fast. All the same it must have been a difficult meeting. However he told her (with perfect truth) that he loved her far more than Eleanor, and he admired little William; and Rosamund was too fond of him to want to make him miserable. So they settled down pretty comfortably; but this time Henry took the precaution of laying out a maze, so that the house at Woodstock was perfectly concealed from jealous eyes. For he had already discovered the savage streak in Eleanor's nature.

Rosamund had another baby after this, another boy, and

Henry went back to Normandy; but he returned to England within a year, for King Stephen died. Then Henry and Eleanor were crowned in Westminster Abbey with great splendour. It was his hour of glory, and no doubt someone described it all to the gentle Rosamund. Perhaps she remembered that conversation in the willow tree, not so very long ago.

Now Henry wondered whether Eleanor wouldn't be easier to live with, if she wasn't quite so clever. She seemed to think she could run his affairs more efficiently than he did, and she had an irritating way of talking down to him, as if he wasn't quite grown-up. All the same he had to keep on the right side of her, because he soon found that her temper was even worse than his own. Not a very hopeful recipe for happy living, but they kept up appearances, and their appearances were extremely splendid.

They circulated between several palaces. This was partly for reasons of hygiene; for the Court was so crowded and the plumbing so primitive, after a few months everyone was glad to move on while the servants set to work scrubbing and airing – 'sweetening', as they called it. Most often they stayed at Westminster, Winchester – and Woodstock.

It was a risk; but the maze was so cunningly contrived that Henry told himself Eleanor would never find Rosamund. He needed the dear girl desperately at this time. She was always smiling, never complained, and wouldn't have dreamt of telling him what to do. Besides, her children were nicely brought up, while Eleanor's were as savage as wolf cubs, and seemed to do nothing but squabble all day. So although Eleanor groaned about it, and told him that Oxfordshire was inhabited exclusively by barbarians, he took no notice; and as she didn't want to be left behind, she had to put up with it. But she began to wonder what on earth her husband was doing, when she knew he wasn't hunting, and messengers on urgent business had to sit kicking their heels all day.

So she watched him. And one afternoon when he came home she saw that a strand of embroidery silk had caught in his spur, and had been unwinding as he walked. She put her foot on it, and the end pulled free before he noticed anything. How simple! All she had to do was follow the silken trail, and discover just what it was that kept him away from home, day after day. But her heart was beating hard, because embroidery silk could only mean one thing – a woman.

The silk led her through the park, between the hazel clumps and the may bushes; and her heart beat hard and her hands winding the silk shook with fury. Certainly she despised Henry, but that didn't mean she was going to give him up to anyone else.

The silk led her to a thicket, and through it along a path so narrow, she would never have discovered it otherwise. And she came to a door in a stout wall. The silk passed under the door, but the door was locked.

Eleanor threw herself on the door, kicking, and beating on it with her clenched fists. Then she rushed back to the palace like a whirlwind. The first person she saw was a gardener; she screamed at him to follow her, and bring an iron bar. The man was frightened because she looked so wild, and hurried after her; when she got down on her hands and knees and started crawling through the thicket, he thought she had gone mad. "Break down the door!" she screamed at him in French when they reached it. "Smash it! At once! or I shall tear you to pieces!" The man was a

Norman, you see; he hardly spoke English, and he knew nothing about Rosamund. He was terrified of the Queen, so he did what she wanted, and Eleanor rushed through.

It seemed sunnier on that side of the wall. The telltale silk led a twisting way, round corners and double bends – until, its fateful work done, it ran out just as the track opened into a pretty little garden, all grass and roses. A beautiful girl sat there, embroidering a tablecloth, and two little boys with large blue eyes just like their mother's, were playing in a sandpit close by."

"How do you know she was embroidering a tablecloth?" asked Vincent.

"Why not?" said Charlotte.

"They didn't have tablecloths then."

"Of course they did, and sandpits. Go on, Simon."

"It was a jolly long piece of embroidery silk," Vincent muttered rebelliously. "I bet it wouldn't really have stretched that far."

"Even Eleanor's proud heart must have suffered a pang, at that innocent scene," Simon went on. "Rosamund turned pale, for although she had never met Eleanor, she knew at once who it was. She got up and curtsied to the ground. Eleanor's face was twisted in a cruel smile, as she walked towards her.

"I have come to drink wine with you," she said, through clenched teeth.

Rosamund hurried into the house to fetch wine. The two little boys said nothing, but they wondered who the nasty lady was, who kept biting her nails – something they were not allowed to do.

Rosamund came back with two brimming glasses. Eleanor took a pearl out of her pocket – she was the sort of woman who always has extra jewels about her, to bribe

people with, or poison them. She dropped it into
Rosamund's glass.

"To friendship," she said, raising her glass with a deadly
glint in her eye.

Now Rosamund had heard all about poisoned jewels
from Sister Cecilia; still she always tried to believe the best
of people, and she could only hope that Eleanor was as
noble in spirit, as she was in blood. So she raised the cup
and drank; but alas, alas! She turned deadly pale and
fell to the ground. The wicked queen gave a screech of
frantic laughter, and the poor little boys burst into tears."

"But what about the man who broke down the door?
Didn't he fetch help?" Charlotte demanded.

"He did his best. After the furious queen rushed through,
he ran back to the palace in a terrible fuss. He was frightened of Eleanor, but he was even more frightened of what
Henry would do to him if he didn't tell him that she
had gone mad. Henry was in council at the time. When
he made sense of the man's jabber, he leapt to his feet immediately and rushed out, and the council followed him
to a man, for they had all heard rumours of the beautiful
Rosamund, and they were dying to have a glimpse of her.

Alas, alas! poor Henry was too late. By the time he
reached the bower where his greatest treasure had for so
long been a willing prisoner, and lifted her in his arms, she
was dead.

Eleanor then went into hysterics of remorse, and in fact
she was terrified that Henry would stab her to the heart
there and then, for she knew what a temper he had, and
he was beside himself with grief. But the noble lords
restrained him. Then, amid universal sorrow, Rosamund's
fair body was taken to the convent at Godstow (which is
near Oxford), and there placed in an elaborate coffin in

front of the high altar; it was draped in a pall of white silk, and covered with a silken canopy, while around it candles were kept burning day and night. And on her tomb was written: 'Non Rosamunda, sed Rosa Mundi' – that means, 'Not Rosamund, but Rose of the World', you know; but it isn't so neat out of Latin."

"What happened to the queen?" asked Charlotte.

"Oh, Eleanor got worse and worse, and made such trouble between Henry and his children, that she had to be kept in prison until he died. But there was nothing sweet about *her* captivity: she used to sign herself: 'Eleanora, by the wrath of God Queen of England'."

"It isn't a true story, though, is it?" Vincent wanted to know.

"Well! Some of it's true. But if I'd only told you those bits, you wouldn't have been very interested. Take the ring, for instance, the ring I told you Rosamund gave to Sister Cecilia.

Fifty years ago that ring was found here, just as I described it. But who can tell whether it ever belonged to Rosamund? What we can say, is that wyverns support both the sapphire, and – you remember, Charlotte – the Clifford coat of arms.

The little boys really existed. Henry took them and had them educated with his own children. William grew into a valiant soldier and a true friend, while Nicholas became Archbishop of York. You can see their tombs in Salisbury Cathedral: Longespee (it means Long Sword) they were called.

Some people say that Rosamund was never at the priory in Cannington. The legend says she was; and it's a fact that her grandmother on her mother's side was a Mohun, and lived at Dunster, so that's a connection.

Certainly her tomb was in front of the high altar at Godstow, for St. Hugh saw it there when he visited the convent some years later. He was scandalised to find the 'hearse of a harlot', as he put it, in such an exalted place, and he told the nuns to move it into the churchyard.

But after St. Hugh died, the faithful nuns gathered Rosamund's bones into a bag of perfumed leather, which they put into a leaden case, and buried in the original place inside the church.''

"Saints are usually snarky; it's a shame," said Charlotte.

"Oh, not at all!" Simon replied, as enthusiastically as ever. "St. Hugh was rather splendid. You know when he was Bishop of Lincoln, he opened his forests to the poor so that they could hunt there. And every week he ate with lepers. He stood up for what he thought was right, even against King Henry. In fact Henry was a pall bearer at his funeral."

"Hallo!" Giles called, striding towards them across the grass. "Sorry I was ages. You must be grinding your teeth at the thought of the picnic in the car, and I forgot to give you the key. Hallo," he nodded and smiled at Simon.

"We've been hearing about Fair Rosamund," Charlotte told him. "And Vincent got to the farm machinery."

"Do you know a good place near here, where we can eat our tea?" Giles asked Simon.

"Why don't you go to Combwich? It's only just up the road, and turn right. Drive through the village till you come out on a green, with the river, the Parrett, on your right. I don't know what the tides are, but it's exciting if the water's coming in, it fairly gallops up there like a race horse!"

"Good idea," said Giles. "Why don't you join us?"

"I really can't; I told my aunts I'd be back for tea –
civilised tea – and that must have been hours ago."

"It's nearly six," said Vincent, showing his watch.

"Oh Lord." Simon jumped up and brushed off the dried
grass. "Still, at least they don't expect me to be punctual."
He shook hands vigorously with the three of them and
started off over the green, but halfway across he couldn't
help turning to shout: "The Vikings raided from the
mouth of the Parrett; can't you imagine it, rushing up
on the tide in their long ships – but I must fly!" and he
did, or at any rate ran, and disappeared into a neat little
house called Acacia Cottage.

So Giles and Charlotte and Vincent had their picnic in
Combwich on the river bank, but the tide was out and it
was mostly mud. But there was a place along the hedge that
was full of butterflies – hundreds of them; and they heard
an old scarecrow woman crying "Hope – hope – hope!"
under the hill, to fetch in the cows.

Tom Cox

HREE merry boys, and three merry boys,
 And three merry boys are we,
  As ever did sing in a hempen string
   Under the gallows-tree.

Francis Beaumont
& John Fletcher

Aunt Jane Dory was the first person to sleep in the new spare room. She came with the jasmine. It flowered suddenly after a night's rain, covering the old walls along the drive with waterfalls of scented white; Alice picked it for the house in armfuls. Aunt Jane extricated herself from the car which had brought her from the station, dropped her handbag which burst, and put her foot in a puddle. Charlotte collected the contents of the bag, which were not at all like the things Alice kept in hers: she found a ball of string and a pruning knife, a hook for picking out hooves, a crimson handkerchief with foxes' heads on it, a miniature bottle of brandy (empty), a bunch of bookies' tickets. The handbag itself was precariously made of knitted squares.

Aunt Jane progressed into the house scattering scarves, gloves (not a pair), hankies (used), hairpins and buttons. There was no loop to hang her mackintosh, so it soon fell to the floor; and Pounce found her hat and nested in it. She propped her shooting stick in a corner and it overbalanced and smashed a pane of glass. She was tall and spare, with twinkling grey eyes, a flattish purplish sort of nose like a helping of blackcurrant fool, and hair like a swatch of dead grass. She had a voice like a hunting horn, and called everybody 'm'dear'.

Aunt Mil hurried down as soon as she arrived. The two old ladies were delighted to see each other, and cut out everyone else. Aunt Mil conducted a tour of the house, pointing out the improvements, while the other Dorys followed mute behind. Aunt Jane smoked Turkish cigarettes one after another, in a long ivory holder, and had a profligate habit of tossing away the smouldering ends that kept Giles on his toes.

"How long is she staying?" he whispered to Alice as they tramped up the grand stair in the empty part of the house.

"Ssh! only three days."

"*Careful!*" he exclaimed, diving to grab Aunt Jane as she missed her footing on the top step.

"Oops a daisy," she said, without looking round, and strode ahead into the ball-room.

"They've put on the slates, Jane," Aunt Mil told her, crowding after. "Not a drop through the ceiling last night although it poured; I came up to look."

Aunt Jane gave a snort of laughter. "Remember the Eight to Eighty, that year there was the thunderstorm? And your ma stood the Chinese bowl in the corner under the leak, and the drips rang out ping, pang, pong! till we thought we should die laughing!"

"What was the Eight to Eighty?" Charlotte wanted to know.

"Oh that was a ball we used to give every year for the

Hunt," said Aunt Mil. "Anyone from eight to eighty could come. Remember old Maud Poorish, Jane?"

"Rather! She'd stuck at eighty for years. All nods and smiles, disintegrating feathers and silk off the shoulders."

"Remember Archy Green? Got a bit sozzled on cup, and wouldn't leave you alone, Jane; kept on at you to marry him."

"Only proposal I ever had. Must have asked me six times that one evening."

So the cousins remembered, and the evening light tenderly rouged their old cheeks.

Vincent joined them at supper. He stared at Aunt Jane with fascination, so that Alice waited on edge for bricks to drop; but luckily his attention was distracted by a cock-chafer he had found, which he had brought secretly to table in a matchbox in his pocket. He could feel it scraping to get out. The butter took a toss between the old aunts, and landed face-down on the carpet. Charlotte noticed, as she picked it up, that Aunt Jane was sitting astride her chair, in a very horsemanlike way. The butter was all furry with fluff and Pouncehairs, and Charlotte spent much of the meal cleaning them off.

When supper was over Aunt Jane asked for a kettle of boiling water, to fill her hot bottle and thermos flask. Then she said goodnight all round, and went upstairs. One or two crashes, that they took to be her unpacking, and a snatch of trumpeting song reached the Dorys in the kitchen, where Alice was ironing and Charlotte and Giles were struggling with homework and accounts.

Vincent shut himself into his bedroom, and emptied out the cockchafer. It was really a splendid sight. It was nearly as long as his thumb, with a nice little fringe, and a face, of a sort, that seemed to grin at him. All of a sudden it zoomed up off the bed and round the room, buzzing and banging until it knocked itself out and crashed onto its back, where it lay helplessly weaving its jointed legs.

There came a startling burst of song from Aunt Jane next door.

"Oh, soldier, soldier, won't you marry me,
With your musket, fife, and dru-um?"

Vincent put the cockchafer back on its feet. His bony fingers were very gentle. Up it dashed again, and repeated its performance until it came to grief, on the bed this time.

"So – *off* she went to the cobbler's shop,
As fast as she could ru-un;
And she bought him boots of the very very best,
And the soldier put them on.
Oh! *Sol*dier, soldier, won't you marry me . . ."

The song gained emphasis as it progressed, and there were sounds of restlessness in the room next door. At the last couplet:

"Oh, no, pretty maid, I cannot marry you,
For I have a wife at home!"

Aunt Jane's voice rose to a perfect screech of triumph. Then abruptly, all was silent.

Vincent moved the beetle onto his pillow. He checked that the window was fastened, and went out, shutting the door with care. In the passage he hesitated, but while he was making up his mind Aunt Jane, who had very sharp ears, cried out: "Come in!" So he did.

She looked smaller in bed. She was wrapped in a crimson shawl, and drinking something steaming out of a toothglass.

"Would you like me to show you my cockchafer?" he asked, with his best social duty manner.

"No."

"What're you drinking?"

"Water, m'dear, just water," Aunt Jane told him firmly. "Hot water, for the kidneys; my medical man insists."

"It doesn't smell like water."

"What does it smell like then, Cleverboots?"

"Gin," he said, catching sight of the bottle on the bedside table.

"*Gin!*" exclaimed Aunt Jane, casting up her eyes to the ceiling. "*Gin!* Oh, perish the thought! It's poison to me, m'dear, gin is – poison; never could keep it down." She took a reassuring swig, beadily eyeing him over the rim of the toothglass. "Sit down," she commanded. He took the edge of a chair.

"I suppose you heard me singing and thought I was tight. Not a bit of it. I sing to keep up my spirits. Now this may look to you like a gin bottle," she went on, adding a little from it to the toothglass. "But it ain't; it's clear spring water with mineral properties, m'dear, that I am obliged to take for my health. I keep it in a gin bottle," she said, tasting from the glass and smacking her lips, "because it looks more cheerful.

But how you remind me of my cousin Harry, sitting there. He was just such a little quick boy as you; and I expect you collect birds' eggs as well as beetles, don't you, m'dear?"

"Not birds' eggs," said Vincent. "At least only sometimes. Dad says it's wrong."

"Oh your father's like my cousin Giles, a foreign stamps and old coins boy. It seems to me there are two sorts of men, m'dear: the attractive sort, that isn't any good; and the good sort that isn't attractive. That's why I'm still single.

Mind you I've a soft spot for a bad lot, as Harry's old

nurse used to say; and if I'd been asked by Charles Stuart, say, or Tom Cox – you've heard of them, I expect?"

"No," said Vincent. He wasn't at ease on the chair; he was ready to dash away. But Aunt Jane wanted to talk, and she played him skilfully, enticing him with crumbs of conversation until at last he wriggled his back into the back of the chair, and sat still and listened.

"We'll forget about Charles the Second because he was only a king, and you're bound to learn about him some day. Tom Cox lived at the same time, and he was a highwayman.

His father was a gentleman in Blandford – that's in Dorset, where I come from, and he was the youngest of the family. He was a beautiful child, and grew up very handsome. His ma spoilt him dreadfully. He was one of those boys who's never out of trouble, but she made no end of excuses for him, and roared even louder than he did every time he got a walloping, so his father soon stopped trying to keep him in order. Still Thomas was so good-looking, and so cheerful and full of high spirits, nobody could help liking him; but his poor old Dad used to shake his head sometimes, and say he feared young Tom was born to be hanged.

The old squire died at last, leaving his widow and children very sorrowful, including Tom who cried heartily for several days. But by and by he remembered that his pa had left him some money. It wasn't much because Tom was the youngest son; but it seemed a lot to him who up till then had never had any of his own. Some exciting new friends turned up – they always do, m'dear – to show him how to spend it, and he bought some smart clothes, and a fiery horse that terrified his mother. In fact he thoroughly enjoyed himself until his fortune had all gone, and he was so much in debt that he had to leave the district.

So he said good-bye to his grief-stricken parent, shedding some tears on her shoulder; ignored his brothers (they were no longer on speaking terms); and set off at a gallop in a characteristic cloud of dust. How was he going to earn his living? Well, he had no ambitions in that direction; being the son of a gent, he had never learnt a trade. But he knew how to cheat at cards; he rode recklessly enough to win races; and he shot straight enough to put the fear of God into an honest man. With these accomplishments it seemed natural to join the Gentlemen of the Road, and sure enough, he hadn't travelled a day's ride from his mother's house when he was startled by a horseman bearing down on him through the mist.

The fellow did not bother to speak, beyond a rough greeting – "Oy there!" or something similar – and hauling in his horse at the last minute, cramming close to Tom, fired his pistol in the air, while he held out an imperious hand for Tom's valuables.

Tom handed over his purse, which only contained one guinea, pressed upon him at parting by his tearful and ever-indulgent ma. The robber tipped it out with a sneer, and gave Tom to understand that it wouldn't do.

"It's all I've got," said Tom apologetically.

The robber levelled his pistol at Tom's head, preparing to blow it off his shoulders.

"No, but wait a bit," our hero said hastily. "Just have a little patience, and if you don't hear something to your advantage, you can kill me then." The robber grumbled, but he was curious; Tom's cocksure manner was not what he was used to. The end of it was that they rode away together to the nearest inn, where they had their meat and drink 'on the house' – this being a convenient arrangement between the landlord and the highwaymen, that they would not damage himself or his property in return for free victuals whenever they were in that part of the country. When they had eaten, they sat down with another bottle to play at cards; and as Tom won every time, the robber had to admit that he was more fly than he looked, and expressed himself willing to a partnership.

Tom did so well, m'dear, that he could have retired on his profits in a year or two, and lived comfortably. But he wasn't that sort of a stick-in-the-mud; he was in it for the kicks as much as the cash, and he never thought about tomorrow, or saved a penny. The more he took, the more he spent, and of course as his habits got more and more expensive, he had to step up his crimes to pay for them. It wasn't just the drink. (Never touch the demon drink, m'dear," warned Aunt Jane with a reflective sip at the toothglass, "for it has brought better men than our hero to a pauper's grave.) As I was saying: it wasn't just the drink, but the horses and clothes and, of course, the girls. He was handsome and dashing and generous with presents, and naturally no female could resist him.

But one fine day he was caught; and the next thing he knew, he was being tried for his life at Gloucester Assizes. His mother hurried there to plead for him, and such were her tears and entreaties, and such the penitence of frightened young Tom, that he was let off with a hefty fine. She took him home, and told everybody he had learned his lesson, and was going to settle down quietly on the estate with his brothers.

But not a bit of it! He soon got over his fright, and then his family bored him to tears. When there was fine company to dinner, his fingers itched after the watches and snuffboxes of the gentlemen, and the jewels of the ladies. He enjoyed making his brothers blush by dropping into thieves' cant, and if he was asked to join in a quiet game of cards after dinner, everybody else soon regretted it. It wasn't long before even his devoted parent was ashamed of him; and when he finally left, taking the best horse in the stable, all the housekeeping money and several of his brothers' suits of clothes, she was not sorry. She took to calling him 'poor Tom', as if he was dead.

This time he knew he had left home for good; and now there was a crazy recklessness about him, as though he really wanted to be hanged – hell-bent, you might have called him. He became a living legend, and he was still so handsome that the ladies sighed as he gallantly removed their diamonds. But the price on his head would have tempted the most lovesick chambermaid; and that was exactly what happened: he was betrayed, caught, and thrown into jail. This time his mother didn't come to the trial; but many women did, and wept at the sight of his beauty and repentance.

Now in those days, if a girl offered to marry a rogue at the gallows, his life was spared. This was Tom's only hope, and he was lucky. He noticed a woman looking fondly at him during the trial, and soon they were exchanging languishing glances. He stared straight at her while the judge condemned him to be hanged, with his big blue eyes full of tears, and his fingers tightly crossed behind his back, and sure enough she came up to scratch and offered herself for his sake. So he was released, and off they went arm in arm, to the cheers of the crowd. And here was another bit of luck: she had a little property of her own, worth fifteen hundred pounds.

He ran through the lot in a year. Maybe he tried to change his ways, but the pull of the old life was too strong. I suppose she thought she could reform him; never fall into that trap, m'dear. You can't change a leopard's spots or the colour of your skin, and if a man's bad at twenty-five he'll be worse at fifty. Anyway, when Tom went back to the road it broke her heart.

The next time he was caught they sent him to Ilchester jail in Somerset. But they forgot that the jailer had a niece, who naturally was all agog when she heard Tom was coming, and fell for him hook, line and sinker. She contrived that he was given a cell of his own, and brought him little treats as he lay there awaiting trial; and one night when her drunken old uncle lay snoring, dead to the world, she stole his keys and let Tom out.

Tom had to creep through the jailer's quarters, where he lay sprawled like a dirty old hound, and he noticed a silver mug standing by the bed. He couldn't resist taking it. He gave the girl some smacking kisses, stole a good horse from a gentleman's stable, and rode off with all speed.

He reached Coventry eventually, where he put up at an inn he knew. It so happened two other highwaymen had the next room, and as the wall between was thin, he heard them boasting that they'd taken over a hundred pounds that day on the road. So he made a plan with himself to relieve them of it. Next morning he set off on his horse, titupping out of the yard like a nice sober middleclass gent; and sure enough since he was well-mounted, and very well-dressed, the two thieves quickly came after.

Tom acted all the time as if he'd no idea what they were up to, but he knew the road, and when he reached a deserted bit of heath he hid in a thicket until they had galloped past. Then he took them completely by surprise, shot one dead, and stuffed his pockets with their hundred pounds."

Aunt Jane yawned, and experimentally tipped the toothglass, but there wasn't a drop left in it.

"Go on," said Vincent. His face and knees gleamed whitely in the gloom.

"Youth and beauty don't last for ever, m'dear, remember that; and when you gamble remember that luck runs out.

Tom Cox was caught for the last time, and it didn't take the judge long to sentence him to death.

His brothers had cut him off, long since. His suffering wife and his poor mother were dead. He was hauled to the gallows in a cart with the chaplain beside him, reading him a sermon and trying to get him to repent. Well, Tom didn't want to be hanged, but he was damned if he was sorry, and the holy man made him so mad, that he kicked him and the hangman both into the crowd, and chucked his own boots after them! So they stood him up in the cart with the rope round his neck, while he desperately searched the faces for one silly soft woman to come to his rescue. But nobody offered to take him on again; and that was the end of him."

"Why did they hang him in a cart?"

"Why the cart stopped under the gallows, and they put the rope round his neck; and then the horse pulled the cart away so he was strung up, don't you see."

Vincent was silent, visualising the scene.

"Shut the window, there's a good chap," said Aunt Jane, shifting to a more comfortable position, and reaching for her thriller on the bedside table. "I see this one's finished," peering into the bottle marked gin as she spoke, and handing it to Vincent. "You might put it into the suitcase over there; I shouldn't like your mother to worry about my health. People so easily get fussed." Vincent did as he was told and noticed that there was another bottle of what Aunt Jane called mineral water among her clothes. But she had found her place in the thriller and started to read.

"Good night, then," he said. She did not answer, only raised her left hand. He slipped out.

He was just going into his room, when he heard Charlotte give a blood-curdling scream. Giles and Alice rushed, but he was closer, and reached her first. She was kneeling on her bed, as white as the sheet.

"*Oh!*" she screamed, "a *horrible*, enormous great beetle came creeping in under the door! *Oh* I do *hate* the country!"

"Where is it?" he asked calmly.

"It's gone. It dashed out of the window."

"You beastly ass!" he cried. "I found it, it was mine!" And he thrust his head and shoulders out of the window, and hung there, mourning.

Midsummer Midnights

Black spirits and white,
Red spirits and grey,
Mingle, mingle, mingle,
You that mingle may.

Thomas Middleton

It was midsummer. The roses at Pippenhay were old, so old that their petals were crumpled and faded. They boasted nothing so gross as a perfume, but had a delicate scent if you put your face close to a flower, and their collective sweetness Alice could smell through her open bedroom window.

Her baby had been born three weeks early. Giles said afterwards that Aunt Jane brought it on; she certainly had a devastating effect on the crockery and furniture.

"Just the same, poor old Jane," Aunt Mil said with satisfaction, after she had gone; and she mended the butter-dish, which turned out, when they finished the butter, to have been broken; stitched some more rings on the spare room curtains; and found another flower pot for the cyclamen.

The baby came in the middle of the night, so easily and quietly and privately, that it seemed like a miracle to Charlotte, who had been secretly worrying in case she had to be an emergency nurse when it was born. It was a boy, and they called him Harry after his Great Uncle Harry, and the bells in the village church were rung for him.

Mrs. Trim came in to look after the house and the new baby. She was a shortish, squattish, past-middle-aged lady, with very lively, slightly bulgy green eyes, a straight nose and a wide, gossipy mouth, and hair still more brown than silver. She had a red complexion and rubbery, thick-calved legs, and went about the house at the double. As for Trim – she wasn't. She bulged between her buttons, and her stripey skirt was done up with a nappy pin, and her slippers were down at heel. Her stockings, as she said herself, were 'more holey than righteous!' But as soon as Alice saw her, she knew she wouldn't drop the baby or upset the children or madden Giles or bustle Aunt Mil, and those were the important things.

Every afternoon, after Alice's rest, Mrs. Trim would come up with a tray of tea and biscuits. Then Alice would feed the baby, or sit him beside her in the bed, and Mrs. Trim would pour tea and talk. She had a way of telling a story that made you feel you were there. It was back to elementals, with Mrs. Trim; her tales had the simple drama of the Old Testament, when black was black and white was white, and the world was as strange as it was beautiful.

"I shall never forget, Mrs. Dory – give me that sweet child, and I'll just get up his wind a minute – the time I was down the garden shutting up my fowls one night. Near Christmas, it must have been, for though not late it was dark; and coming out I saw a snow white lamb just standing there and perfect every detail. Now it can't have been more than a fortnight after, that the police knocked at my door, and I'd to go to the hospital, for my poor brother-in-law, that was husband to my sister Ivy, had been caught up in the machinery at his work, and she was that upset, I had to identify the body."

"How frightful!" said Alice.

"Oh, it was. Look at him trying to sit! I don't think I ever saw such a strong baby! But it's quite different now to what it was, the rearing of young children; it's much better. Why, mother kept us all in long frocks till we were a year old; think of the washing! And never any freedom for their darling legs," exhibiting Harry's as she spoke.

"We'd to walk three miles to school, and three miles back, summer and winter. Well, we were fortunate; we had enough to eat, and we were warmly dressed, mother saw to all that. But some of the children! Mrs. Dory, it would have made your heart bleed to see the older ones grasping the little ones in their arms, to try and keep them from the cold! Of course it was all lovely in summer; but in winter it was very hard. Children used to die of the scarlet fever, or diphtheria; but you're too young to remember all that."

Alice lay with half-closed eyes, content to drink tea and share the baby. She did not need to speak; Mrs. Trim would soon take up the thread again, or start another.

"It isn't surprising, some of the old customs people used to believe in; all twaddle, you'd call it most likely. Not that father would ever have let us go in for anything like that; but I remember my sister Lily writing out all the letters in the alphabet, on little pieces of paper, and putting them face downwards in a bowl of water on Midsummer Eve. Next morning she was up first for once, and ran to the bowl to see if any of the letters had turned up, which would be the initials of her future husband. Now there was one boy, Billy Small, that she detested; so my brother

Dick, him that's a farmer now over Langport way, had turned up the B and the S in the night! How Lily did cry, when she found it, and how we all roared! Take back the baby a minute, Mrs. Dory, and I'll give you more tea."

Alice stretched out her arms and bedded Harry snugly beside her. Mrs. Trim poured tea, considering.

"There's a funny old idea about going to church at midnight on a Midsummer's Eve. I've never done it myself, mind – father would have killed me if I had; and people nowadays would think it all nonsense I expect. I'll make a story of it to amuse you. I used to like telling stories to my younger sisters: specially the ghosty sort, like this one. But you can't expect Ernest – that's my husband – to be interested in such things. It was a grief to me that I never had any children.

Imagine then it was Midsummer's Eve, and the end of a lovely hot day. They had been hauling in the hay, and the air still smelt of it. It was so still, you could hear the river at the bottom of the valley. The moon set off like a little white sail on its journey across the sky.

There was only one light left burning in the village, and that was in the cobbler's shop. All day he'd been busy, tap tap tap, as if he was making coffins. Now he had stopped work, but his wife was sitting up with the baby, who was sickly, poor little thing.

The shop door opened, and the cobbler came out into the street. He was still a young man, but lame, and bent with hunching over boots all day, and he looked much older than he was. He set off up the street towards the church, which loomed among its yews at the top of the hill. He kept well into the shadow of the hedge, and if he had to cross a patch of moonlight, he scuttled over it as if he didn't want to be seen.

Some rough steps led up the bank into the bottom of the churchyard, and he went that way. He looked once over his shoulder. He could see his wife with the baby in the cottage window: thinking about him, perhaps. The fields had a watery, silvery wash of moonlight; it was all kind and calm. He could hear the cows pulling at the grass in the meadow alongside the churchyard.

He crept between the tombstones to the church porch and crouched there, hugging his knees. His hands and feet were clammy, though the air was warm; he had to clench his teeth to stop them from chattering. The coldness of death was in his bones.

He hadn't got a watch, but he could tell the time by the moon. He had never learnt the fancy names of the stars, though they were friends he had known all his life; he glanced up at them now and then, as he waited there. High above him the weather vane gleamed in their light, and looked as if it might flap its wings and crow.

On the stroke of midnight the church bell began to toll. The cobbler caught his breath. He was too scared to move, but he turned his eyes towards the churchyard. It was filling with the shades of men and women. Some had children with them, some carried babies in their arms. These were not the ghosts of the dead – they were all people he knew, the people in the village now lying asleep. And the church door was opening slowly, soundlessly beside him.

The shadows of the villagers flowed up the path and in at the gaping door. He whispered the name of each one as it passed. Strangely intent ghosts they were, with no humanity between them, though mothers and children were hand in hand. There was the squire with his wife and daughters in their silks; the doctor with his ghostly coat unbuttoned and his ghostly hair awry, as though he had just got in from hunting; there were the deaf and dumb twins, old maids; the crippled poacher with his snares flap flapping from his belt, and the boy with the clappers who scared the crows. There was the smith in his strength, the miller in his richness, the idiot in his poverty: every soul in the parish passed him on its way into church; and there was his own pretty wife, carrying their little daughter in her arms, and himself limping along beside them – he had never hobbled so easily as he did that night, gliding over the stones.

The bell was silent, and the great door slowly closed. Presently he heard the gloomy sound of the organ inside the church; and when it stopped, the murmur of the congregation in prayer. A hymn was sung. How weird and wild that ghostly singing seemed! He waited in the porch as if he had been turned to stone, a little, thin, ugly man; as if one of the monsters carved on the tower had come down and was cowering there. But his heart was beating hard with dread. For whoever failed to leave the church when the ghostly service was done, that man or woman – or child – would be dead within the year.

At last the last hymn was sung, and in the following silence, the great door swung open once more. The ghosts streamed out. His eyes flickered fearfully from face to face. Where was the squire's second daughter, the gentle one? And poor Margaret, who was only married last week – her husband left the church alone. He stared desperately at the wraiths as they passed him and vanished in the churchyard. Only a few left – ah, what was this? Himself – alone! Alone! without wife or daughter! He rushed among the ghosts, he struggled desperately to force his way into the church – but it was no use. The great door was closing; he heard the click of the latch as he threw himself upon it, beating the unfeeling timber until his knuckles bled.

Next morning when the sun was shining, and the birds were singing their hearts out, the sexton came to open the church for Sabbath prayer. He found the poor cobbler still in the porch. He had lost his wits from grief."

"What an idiot I am," said Alice, wiping at her eyes. "Mrs. Trim, your story has made me cry."

"Oh that's because you're all over emotional after the baby," said the smiling nurse. She liked a good listener. "Still it is pathetic, I agree."

"Tell me something else to cheer me up."

"Well, I don't know – Mr. Dory will think I ought to have better things to do, than sit here yarning all afternoon! Let me see. There's the tale of the old Widow Leakey, that used to live at Minehead. Her son was in the shipping business between there and Waterford – which I believe to be in Ireland, but you'll know for certain. She was a wonderful agreeable old lady, and her friends all used to say, what a shame it was that such a charming person should ever die. To this she always answered very straight, that they would not enjoy her company so much after she was dead, and so it turned out. For her ghost appeared often, both on sea and on land, and her character had changed; she had turned into a horrible surly old woman, and once kicked her doctor when she met him in a field, because he was not quick enough at handing her over a stile! I suppose he thought now she was a ghost, she would be content to go through it.

The sailors and fishermen at Minehead grew to dread her visits, for she often appeared on the quay, when she would whistle for a boat. But she had some dark power over the weather, for so soon as her whistle was heard, a storm would rise up on the instant; and then woe betide anybody who was out at sea! And that was how she ruined her son's trade, for she acted as if he was no child of hers, and did terrible damage to his shipping.

One evening when his wife was dressing for dinner, she was horrified to see, in her mirror, her dead mother-in-law's face looking over her shoulder. However she kept her wits about her, and got rid of the old woman by sending her off to visit a wicked Irish priest, to tell him to repent at once and mend his ways, or he would die on the gallows. But he was so bad, he took no notice of old Mrs. Leakey; for he said if he was born to be hanged, at least he wouldn't be drowned!''

"Do you believe these stories yourself, Mrs. Trim?'' asked Alice, who had been watching her face.

"Do I believe them? Goodness, I don't know how to answer that one!

I suppose I could say that I've experienced so much in my life, I never could actually *dis*believe in them. People used to be so sure of such things – of devils and angels and fairies and ghosts – it makes you think there must be something in it. Then I dream. I dream something strange, and it doesn't worry me; but all day I'll think on, and think on, and sooner or later the meaning of it'll come into my mind, I'll have my dream out.

There's things I wouldn't do. I wouldn't sit down thirteen at table, I wouldn't walk under a ladder. I wouldn't dance after midnight on a Saturday night.''

"I know about not having thirteen people round a table, and not walking under ladders; but I'm sure I've danced after twelve on Saturday – what's wrong with that?''

"What, dance into Sunday!'' said Mrs. Trim, quite

shocked. "Now that's something I've never done, not in all my life. Oh, I can tell you a story about that – if you're interested in my yarns, as my husband calls them.

Tom and Emily were married on Midsummer Day, in the village of Stanton Drew. That's between Bath and Bristol, on the river Chew; it was only a tiny place then, and everyone in the village went to the church, and then they just sat down on the grass outside the inn, and dishes of cold food and jugs of cider were handed round. It was beautiful weather, and the old folks, and the babies, soon dropped off to sleep in the sun; but the rest found plenty to talk about, even though they saw each other every day, and they kept the cider jugs circulating.

Everyone knew Emily, and everyone loved her; she was the prettiest girl in the parish, and full of high spirits. Now she was pestering the old village fiddler to give them a tune to dance to. At last she had her way, and he hobbled out, and fitting his fiddle under his chin he started with Sellenger's Round. All the young men and maids stood up at once, and Emily and Tom had a chance to dance with all the sweethearts they might have chosen before each other. So they went on to Strip the Willow and Petronella, and when the sun went down they were still dancing.

Now the housewives had long since gone home to get supper, and their husbands to milk the cows; the children had been called in, and the rooks were flying back to their nests in the elms around the church. So at last Tom and Emily and their friends flopped down, laughing, on the grass, and ate ham and pickles with their fingers, and drank mug after mug of cider.

Then some began to talk of going home; but Emily wouldn't hear of that. She and Tom had to live with his parents, as they couldn't afford a place of their own, and she was in no hurry to get back to her mother-in-law. So she said it was a shame to break up the party when they'd only just started to enjoy themselves; and she kept the fiddler filled to the brim with cider, so he agreed to go on playing after supper. It was a lovely evening for a dance. The grass was springy under their feet, the warm air smelt of dog roses and honeysuckle, and over their heads a thousand stars were pricking out one by one.

But the tinny church clock across the fields struck midnight at last, and the old man put away his fiddle. This didn't suit Emily, who was having the time of her life; but even she couldn't make him play any longer. He said it was a sin to dance on the Sabbath, and he wouldn't be a party to it; and he hobbled away to the tiny cottage where he lived. So the young people hung about at a loss, though one or two of them perhaps agreed with the fiddler, and would have liked to be home in bed.

"Darned old fool!" cried Emily, losing her temper. "Why can't any of you play the fiddle?" she demanded, looking angrily round. "I'd do anything for a fiddler, I'd give him anything he asked. I tell you, I'd go to hell itself, if I could get a fiddler from there!" Here Tom put his arm round her, but she shook herself free. "I would, I tell you! There's nothing worse than to be stopped in the middle of a dance, because some darned old fool says – " here she imitated the old man's voice – "'tis a wicked sin, to go dancing into the Lord's Day! As if the Lord cared!" she added, with a sarcastic laugh.

"Hush, though, Em'ly," said Tom in a low voice, pointing across the grass, and they all stared. For a little old man was approaching through the darkness, with an instrument under his arm. At first they thought it was the village fiddler, come back for more cider and another tune after all. "His wife has locked him out!" cried Emily, and they all burst out laughing.

But as the old man drew near they saw that he was a stranger. He was trimly dressed, and had a small pointed beard. He bowed politely to Emily, and offered to play for the dancing; he did not speak in the dialect of those parts. Emily was taken aback, and nudged Tom to answer; but that would not do: the bargain had to be made with Emily, or the old man wouldn't play. And it seemed to them all that the night had turned suddenly cold.

"All right then! Give us a tune, Grandpa!" And shaking out her skirts Emily stood up with Tom, and the young men and girls joined them. So the old gentleman started to play. But the tune he played was so slow and solemn that in a few minutes Emily called out: "What's this – the Snail's Funeral? 'Tis a wedding we're at, remember!" And they all cheered, and stamped their feet.

"As you wish," said the old man, and this time the tune was too quick almost, even for Emily. They were soon laughing with excitement, and by and by they cried out for him to stop, so that they could get their breath. But he seemed to be deaf, this old fiddler; he only went on playing faster and faster, and the dreadful thing was that they could not stop dancing, although soon their breath was coming so hard that the tears ran down their cheeks with the pain of it, and they felt the muscles in their legs would crack. Still he played, and still they must dance; and now to their horror, when they caught a glimpse of him, they saw that his neat suit had shagged into goat hair, and he had got two horns on his head, and his polished shoes had turned into cloven hooves. And it was no good crying for mercy, for still he played on and on, and kept them whirling about him.

He played until the first cock crowed. Then he dropped his fiddle, and bent his stern gaze upon them as they stood gasping in a circle around him. "I leave you," he said, in a voice of thunder, "as a monument to your wickedness and my power!" His words made them cold all through; and the world turned still, and grey, and silent.

There was bitter grief in the village that morning. The old fiddler led the way to the place of the dance, and there they found all that was left of the wedding party: one of Emily's little blue shoes in the hedge, and a grim circle of standing stones, in what had been empty grass."

"Heavens!" said Alice. "I shall think twice before I go dancing into Sunday again!"

"How I do run on!" exclaimed Mrs. Trim, returning to the present with a smile, and beginning to stack the cups. "You'd talk the hind leg off a donkey, that's what Ernest says to me, and really you have to give him credit for it.

Now pass me that darling baby a minute, and I'll change him, and then I'll just get the nappies out on the line and these few dishes washed, and put on the kettle. The children'll be home for their teas any minute.

Look at him now, Mrs. Dory!" displaying the baby wriggling in interrupted sleep. "Look at him trying to hold up his head already! Isn't he strong for a fortnight? He'll walk within a twelvemonth for certain! I don't know when I've ever seen such a strong baby!"

She handed back Harry, whitely parcelled, and his eyes beaded to and fro, very disgruntled; but then he focused on his mother's dear face, and Alice thought he smiled.

Saint Wulfric

FOR Mercy has a human heart,
Pity a human face,
And Love, the human form divine,
And Peace, the human dress.

William Blake

The church dedicated to Saints Simon and Jude had watched over Pippenhay village for more than a thousand years. Its yews sheltered the bones of all the local families, including generations of Dorys; and thither every Sunday trudged Aunt Mil, following the family footpath across the fields in her hat like a brown bowl. Bad weather only added a challenge, and put an edge to her voice in the hymns which she always sang full throttle, regardless of 'Choir Only' or 'pp' directions'.

Charlotte went with her. She hadn't bothered much about church in London, which seemed impersonal in spite of the efforts of the cheery vicar; but here she felt at home. Her great-great-grandmother's likeness smiled down from the stained glass window dedicated to Saint Anne; the prayer book she used had her grandfather's initials in gold on the cover. She took the plunge and joined the choir.

Giles was waiting for them with the car that Sunday

because it had begun to pour. Mr. Jairus the parson came up to speak to them.

"I hear you have a new arrival," he said. "Congratulations!"

"Thanks," said Giles. "Come back with us, and have a glass of sherry to celebrate."

"I'd like to, very much," said Mr. Jairus. "Can I follow on later? I won't be long."

"Of course," said Giles, and Aunt Mil and Charlotte got into the car, and the sonorous vicar strode away up the churchyard to greet the remaining congregation, his baldness gleaming in the rain.

Alice put on a bedjacket and Charlotte changed Harry into his best. The sherry and biscuits were arranged on a tray in the bedroom, and Aunt Mil had just got round with a duster when they heard the front door bell, and a minute later Giles ushered in the vicar.

He was a very professional visitor. He soon had them all at ease with a flow of small talk, of which 'splendid' was the operative word. It was a splendid house, and a splendid room, and Alice looked perfectly splendid; the baby was a splendid little fellow, and how splendid it was to see three generations living together in harmony. Aunt Mil might not have liked that last remark, but she was trying to open a packet of biscuits and didn't hear it.

"I hear you've been doing splendid things to the house," Mr. Jairus remarked to Giles. He sipped his sherry and stared round the room, thinking to himself that it must be as cold as the grave half the year.

"I can't say I'm looking forward to our first winter," said Alice, as if she had read his thought. "Well, if I get too cold, I shall simply go to bed. We've got an electric blanket."

"Nonsense!" said Giles. "This isn't like London; you'll find there won't be any time for huddling about in the house trying to keep warm!"

"I shall huddle if I want to," Alice told him. "And so will Harry, and Aunt Mil."

"What it is to be young and active," said Mr. Jairus with a peace-making gesture. "You don't feel the cold at your time of life. I wish I didn't. Unfortunately I have to spend so much of my time indoors, concocting a sermon, or trying to sort out my lamentable accounts; and then you see my father was a parson, and it still gives me the shivers to remember our rectory in Yorkshire. The cold there was frightful, quite frightful."

Vincent came in, and on being reminded, shook hands with Mr. Jairus. He said: "Can I have some sherry?"

"No," said his father.

"Charlotte is!"

"Half a glass, and she's two years older."

"Take some biscuits," said Aunt Mil.

"I really think those old vicarages were built on the principle that bodily suffering is next to godliness," Mr. Jairus went on. "Enormously high ceilings – huge windows whistling with draughts – icy passages – flagstones in the kitchen – it was penitential in those days, honestly: penitential!"

"I suppose that was how the holy men used to live," said Giles. "Hermits and saints, I mean, and people of that sort."

"Perhaps; but the bishop wouldn't have liked it if one had behaved like a saint or a hermit. Some of them were pretty odd. Say my father had copied St. Wulfric, and sat in a cold bath every morning until he had recited the whole of the psalter – it would have had an awful effect on parish affairs, besides giving him pneumonia!"

"Who was St. Wulfric?" asked Charlotte.

"One of our local chaps; lived near Crewkerne."

"Have some more sherry," said Giles, filling the vicar's glass as he spoke.

"Tell about St. Wulfric and his oddness," said Alice. "Pass me Harry, Charly – you don't mind if I feed him, do you, Mr. Jairus?"

"Not a bit," he said, smiling. He finished the biscuit he was eating, and leant back in his chair by the window, with his elbows on its arms and his glass in both hands, and his gaze fixed on a cobweb at the top of the curtains. The spiders enjoyed the curtains at Pippenhay because they were hardly ever drawn.

"Wulfric was born at a place called Contona: Compton Martin it's called now, a few miles out of Bristol. His parents were middling sort of folk, not poor, but certainly not rich. They thought the world of him. He was a most likeable chap, cheerful and easy going, fond of hunting and hawking and drinking and girls; a good friend, and great fun at a party. As soon as he was a man he took holy orders, but that must have been to please his mother, because he wasn't a bit the kind of person you'd expect to sort out your religious problems, and he was very casual about his duties to start with.

One morning he scrambled through his prayers even faster than usual, because he wanted to spend the rest of the day hunting. Someone had lent him a fiery black mare, so he cut quite a figure in his best clothes, and tore after the hounds leaping hedges and ditches in great style. He was dashing through a wood when he caught sight of a beggar limping along the track. He was having such a wonderful day himself, and the old man looked so miserably poor, that he drew in the mare, and fumbled in his belt. He found a couple of silver coins and threw them down to the beggar. "God be with you, my friend!" he called cheerfully, preparing to gallop away. But the beggar looked up at him sternly.

"Aye, maybe," he said. "But God be not with thee."

Wulfric was taken aback, and a little hurt by his ingratitude.

"Thou canst not buy salvation," said the old man, and with that he handed back the money, and pulling his old brown cloak more closely round him, continued on his way.

Wulfric shrugged his shoulders, pushed the silver back in his belt, and galloped off to join his friends. But the joy had gone out of the day.

People were just as superstitious then as they are now, and Wulfric was haunted by the idea that the old man was not really a beggar at all, but a Holy One returned to earth to warn him of his wickedness, before it was too late. For the first time in his life he felt anxious about his immortal soul. When he handed back the mare to his friend after the day's sport, he already knew that he would never hunt again. He made an excuse, and instead of joining the others for a jolly beery evening, he went home and spent most of the night on his knees.

As the first light streaked the sky in the east, Wulfric made an act of renunciation. He was going to forsake the world, and live from that moment a life of penance. By the time his kindly mother came bustling downstairs to supervise the cooking of his breakfast, he had given away his smart clothes and all his money; and he told her he had already taken what he needed: a small loaf of plain brown bread, and a mug of water.

His mother was so proud of him that she immediately visualised him in a stained glass window with 'S. WULFRIC' underneath in capitals. But it was different when he began putting his ideals into practice. She was hurt when he gave the linen shirts she had made him with her own hands to the poor, and embarrassed when he dressed in sackcloth. She was furious when he refused the meat and vegetables cooked just as he liked them, and sent back the wine she had bought specially. She was prepared to argue the matter on a theological plane: since God made the fruits of the earth, she said, it was right to enjoy them; it was a sin of pride to refuse. But Wulfric had made up his mind, and nothing she could say would alter it.

At last she made so many scenes that he left home, and went as chaplain to Sir William Fitzwalter, who was lord of the town where he was born. But the knight was an old friend, and there were too many distractions: it was all second helpings – have some more wine – move closer to the fire – with him. This caused the holy Wulfric such distress that at last Sir William noticed it.

"Nothing worrying you, my dear fellow, is there?" he asked one morning in his bluff but kindly way. "Blowed if you haven't lost weight since you've been here. (Wish I could,)" he added to himself.

"Not enough!" exclaimed the agonised chaplain.

"But my dear chap, you don't want to get any thinner! There's some nasty bugs about – sweating sickness, Job's boils, spring fever, to name only a few; you must look after yourself, or you'll go down like a ninepin."

So Wulfric told him then about his desires and resolutions; and when Sir William understood, his honest heart was fired with admiration. He longed to help his valiant friend in his struggle against the powers of darkness; and he suddenly remembered that at Haselbury Plucknett, where he himself had a manor house, there was an anchorite's cell attached to the church that had fallen vacant.

"Fellow lived in it for years – funny old boy – holy as a cassock but a bit tricky to handle if you know what I mean; habit of giving hellfire sermons at unfortunate times like Christmas or weddings – anyhow he died the other day. Not surprising – cold, draughty, cramped little hole, uncomfortable as purgatory – suit you to a tee."

So Wulfric went to Haselbury Plucknett, and lived in the cell against St. Michael's church, where he worked out for himself a rule of incredible severity. He fasted until his body was little better than a skeleton; he ate nothing but oaten bread and water gruel, which his servant fetched from the monks of nearby Montacute. He had no bed, and so that he should be aware even while he slept of the sins of the world, he lay with his head propped against the wall. And he wore a hair shirt day in, day out, whose constant pricking was very tormenting."

"Did he only have one hair shirt?" asked Vincent.

"Certainly. A rule as strict as that would never allow for a change of clothes."

"It must have got jolly dirty."

"Dirt was all part of the mortification of the saint," said Mr. Jairus firmly. "And remember the cold baths I mentioned earlier. He took one every day, and stayed in it until he had recited the psalter, so that must have had a cleansing effect on his body as well as his soul.

Sir William gave him a coat of mail, but it wasn't much good at first, because it came down to his knees and prevented him from genuflecting. "I'll send it up to London to my armourer, and get him to shorten it for you," the generous knight suggested.

"Too much trouble and expense," said Wulfric briskly. "Let's do it ourselves. You can cut the links, while I pray."

"Cut the links! What with?"

"Why, scissors, of course!" As Sir William stared, Wulfric added impatiently: "You must have a pair of scissors, surely, up at the manor!"

So Sir William borrowed a pair of his lady's scissors; but he didn't tell her what he wanted them for. He brought them back to the cell, and both men knelt, Wulfric in prayer, while Sir William, very red in the face, made a snap at the hem of the coat. To his astonishment the scissors cut through the links as if they were made of cloth; and the divine shortening only failed once because Wulfric, in his excitement at the miracle, interrupted his prayers to see how it was progressing. A crowd gathered outside the cell and collected the miraculous links as they fell; and it was soon discovered that these were better than any medicine to the sick, for they worked many wonderful cures.

It was not to be expected that the devil would allow the holy Wulfric to possess his sanctity in peace. He tortured him with spiritual temptations, and sent his wicked spirits to beat him when he was kneeling at his prayers."

"What's spiritual temptations?" Vincent interrupted again.

"Women," said Charlotte.

"Not women," said Giles. "Feelings that you're holier than anybody else, that sort of thing." He noticed that Aunt Mil had gone to sleep in her chair, and slightly drew the curtain to shield her face from the light. The baby, pinkly bursting with milk, made a small explosion.

"Rude boy," said Charlotte. "What happened then, Mr. Jairus?"

"Wulfric learnt a lot about the devil from his own unpleasant experiences, and so he found he could help people who were sick in their minds, as well as bodies. His fame spread far and wide, and sufferers of all sorts travelled great distances to visit him. But perhaps the greatest miracle of all was this: in spite of the freezing baths, in spite of the pangs of indigestion and the constant chafing of the hair shirt or the coat of mail, Wulfric was never impatient with his visitors. He gave them excellent advice in kind and agreeable language, and that in itself was a valuable lesson in holiness.

One poor fellow who had sold himself to the devil when he was a young man, became haunted by the thought of the fiery tortures awaiting him, and desperate to save his soul at all costs. His wife begged him to go to Wulfric and ask for exorcism, and at last he set off, though he was afraid that the enemy of souls would find a way of preventing him from reaching the saint. Sure enough, as he was fording the stream on the outskirts of Haselbury, the devil dragged him under the water, grasping him tightly to drown him. But Wulfric by heaven's grace knew what was going on, and he had already sent his own confessor to meet the pilgrim, armed with a crucifix and a glass of holy water. As soon as this was sprinkled over the drowning man, the devil with an unearthly screech let him go; and so the poor sinner was brought safely to the saint, who heard his confession, and told him to go in peace.

People were always trying to give him presents, but it wasn't easy to get him to accept them. Feed the hungry and clothe the naked, was his usual brisk advice, and usually they had to make do with that. But a boy was once asked to take him three loaves of plain brown bread. Now he was a stranger there, and hadn't heard much about Wulfric; but he knew that times were hard. He was hungry himself more often than not, and he thought three loaves were too many for the holy man, so on the way he hid two of them.

Wulfric was so grateful when he gave him the single loaf that the boy felt rather ashamed; however, he said nothing and hurried hungrily back to the place where he had hidden the rest of the bread. He was frightened when he looked in, for there was nothing there but two smooth, round stones! He plucked up his courage and took them to the saint, and said he was sorry. Wulfric smiled; a little repentance was as good as a feast to him, and he said some prayers. The stones turned back into bread in front of the astonished boy, and Wulfric gave them to him, with his blessing.

What else about Wulfric? He was a prophet: he foretold the death of Henry I, and he knew that Stephen would be king. Stephen shook his head with a smile, and said the holy man must have mistaken him for somebody else.

"It is no error," Wulfric replied. "It is you, Stephen, that I mean – for the Lord has delivered the realm into your hands. Protect the Church! Defend the poor!"

And now his anxious friends begged him to take better care of himself, for he was growing old; but he wouldn't take any notice. If someone knitted him a blanket he would thank them kindly; but it was sure to appear tucked round a poor woman's baby, within a day or two. His cell was so draughty that on windy nights his candle kept blowing out. But the angels loved him so much that they filled the adjacent church with a heavenly radiance, that shed its beams into his cell. The parish priest, Father Osbern, saw the church windows lit as though flames were burning behind them; he knew it was the glory of angels and saints, and did not dare to go any closer than the cemetery wall.

At last Wulfric called for his confessor. "I must die," he said, "next Saturday," and he made his dispositions, gave comfort and healing, and blessed his friends. And so he died, leaving his people heartbroken.

But as soon as the news of his death reached Montacute, a party of monks set off for Haselbury, armed with staves and cudgels, to demand his body. Father Osbern speedily locked up the church where Wulfric was still lying in an open coffin; and then he came out to meet them. The monks told him that they had fed the anchorite, so they had a right to his mortal remains; besides, Wulfric had promised them his body. "And we aren't going away without it!" one of them declared, brandishing his stave.

By this time an angry crowd of villagers had gathered, so Father Osbern left them on guard while he hurried to Crewkerne to fetch help. Returning to the village as fast as he could, he was dismayed to hear a noise like a zoo or a football match, vague roarings punctuated with shouts and howls; and as he approached the church he saw to his horror that the monks had unbricked the window in the holy cell and were about to kidnap the saint, regardless of Christian decency, and the stones and furious abuse hurled at them by the people of Haselbury. Fortunately when the monks saw Father Osbern and the band of strong men he had brought from Crewkerne and round about, they were somewhat abashed, and finding themselves outnumbered they agreed to leave Wulfric where he was for the time being, until Robert, Bishop of Bath had settled the matter.

So Haselbury kept its saint. He was buried simply in his

cell – no other place seemed good enough; and then it was sealed so that no profane feet should walk there. But later the remains were transferred to a secret grave inside the church, somewhere near the altar. And from that time a side aisle in St. Michael's church at Haselbury Plucknett has been called after St. Wulfric."

"Those Montacute monks were a lot of thugs," said Alice. "It's a pity there's so often a wrangle over the remains of saints."

"Like Fair Rosamund," said Charlotte.

"She wasn't a saint," said Vincent.

"Nearly. You only heard half the story."

"I must be going home," said Mr. Jairus, glancing at his watch. "It's been splendid meeting you all. I'm afraid I talk too much," he thought of adding. His joints cracked like squibs when he got up because he had sat so long. "Don't move, any of you. I can find my own way down."

"No, I'll show you out," said Giles, following him to the door. "You might get lost."

Charlotte and Vincent went with them, whilst Aunt Mil, who had been roused by the disturbance, explained to Alice that she had only closed her eyes for a moment because changeable weather always made her feel tired.

The rain had stopped, and the sparrows were enjoying the puddly drive. Charlotte and Vincent watched from the porch as Mr. Jairus bicycled away, his grasshopper legs like slow clockwork.

Kings and Heroes

The Hero can be Poet, Prophet, King, Priest or what you will, according to the kind of world he finds himself born into.

Thomas Carlyle

The weather was hot, but not broiling; you wouldn't expect, on a weekday, the worst of the holiday traffic; and someone had given Aunt Mil three tickets for an organ recital in Bath Abbey. So Harry and Pounce were left with Mrs. Trim, and Aunt Mil, Alice and Charlotte dressed for a musical afternoon; while Giles and Vincent wore more casual clothes, suitable for a tour of the American Museum and, they hoped, tea.

Aunt Mil had friends in Bath, and she was going to stay with them after the concert. Her small suitcase, neatly packed with a few clothes in a great deal of tissue paper, was safely locked in the boot of the car, and she was wearing her weddings hat, not a bowl but more of a dish, with a little bunch of partridge feathers dead centre on a band, like a school badge. Under it her face had a school-girl expression of innocent excitement; it was some years since she had been able to visit her friends, who were as old as she was.

They took the road across Sedgemoor, and passed a sign-post to Athelney on the right. "Isle of Nobles," Aunt Mil told them from her seat in front. "In King Alfred's day it was a forest completely surrounded by marshes. No-one could get to Athelney except by boat, and Alfred hid there while he was fighting the Danes; this was the only part of England that was loyal to him."

"Was that where he burnt the cakes?" asked Vincent.

"Yes, in Denwulf's hut."

"How does anybody know his name was Denwulf? It might've been Frig or Brod or Eggwhisk, how does anybody know?"

"Because someone called Asser gives an account of it as King Alfred told it to him, and soon the story was being sung in Latin verse, and it is one of the first things we learn in history; every child in England knows that King Alfred burnt the cakes. Even you, Vincent," Aunt Mil added waspishly.

Vincent muttered about assers, but low so that only Charlotte heard him.

"Are you sure you're right about Asser?" Giles asked Aunt Mil. "I didn't think that particular source was as old as that."

"I believe so." Aunt Mil sounded rather offended, so Giles said no more. Presently she went on: "The people round here must have dreaded the Danes. At Aller – that's further over towards Langport – there is a legend about a terrible dragon that used to devour the herds and flocks, and carry off the maidens. But don't you think the dragon was really the Danish longships? Can't you imagine them gliding up the river at night, hissing between the reeds?"

They were crossing the bridge over the Parrett as she

spoke. Beyond it a funny little hill, like a rough for Glastonbury Tor, rose straight up out of the moor.

"That's Burrow Mump," said Aunt Mil. She loved to instruct, and a car journey provided her with a captive audience. "That's a ruined church on the top, dedicated to St. Michael. Churches on hills very often are dedicated to him, I don't know why."

"Perhaps people thought that being an archangel, he'd take a special interest in them," Giles suggested.

"Perhaps," Aunt Mil agreed, but coolly.

"But I was telling you about Athelney, and how King Alfred hid there after he had been defeated in a frightful battle against the Danes. He had with him a gallant company of faithful friends, and they were all used to hardships, but even so the Isle of Nobles was a very bleak and desolate place. In winter it flooded and froze; in warm weather diseases bred in the marshes all round, so men died as easily there as they had under arms. And everyone got jumpy imagining Danes creeping up on them through the trees.

One wet cold windy night, when most of his companions were still out hunting, the king was taking the opportunity to read when his servant, old John, came bustling in.

"There's a nasty old beggar at the door," he said. "Some Dane in disguise, most likely; and come to think of it his accent is certainly odd."

"What does he want?" asked the monarch-without-a-kingdom, without raising his eyes from his book.

"Why bread, of course," said old John, rather sharply. He couldn't read himself, and often said he didn't see the point of it.

"Then we must give him some," said the patient king.

"What! feed a spy?"

"You don't know that he is a spy."

"But we've only the one loaf left; little enough for ourselves; how do you expect me to feed our poor lads when they come back from hunting?"

"John, John," said Alfred wearily – he was extremely tired, and the chilly damp of Athelney made his bones ache – "you must put your trust in Him Who fed the five thousand with five loaves and two fishes. And for His sake you must feed this beggar."

John had no answer to this, and he went away, feeling ashamed, and gave the beggar the last loaf. He was only going to give him half of it, but the poor man was so pleased, he had not the heart to divide it. And a little later the hunting party came back, and they had had unexpected luck, so everyone feasted on roast swan that night, and a dish of carp.

But Alfred stayed by the fire, and his friends left him in peace, because they understood that sometimes he needed to be alone. And by and by he fell into a deep sleep, and he had a dream. He dreamt that an old, old man had come into the room: Alfred knew in his dream that he was very old, although his hair was black. He was wearing rich vestments, a mitre was on his head, and in his right hand he clasped the book of the Gospels. Alfred fell on his knees, and the aged man blessed him. And the room filled with holiness and peace.

"I am called Cuthbert, the servant of Christ," the saintly visitor told him. "To me didst thou give bread. Rejoice and be glad, my son, for from this day I shall be thy protector. Rise up early in the morning, and sound thy horn thrice, and thou shalt have five hundred men prepared for battle." With this the saint vanished; and Alfred woke as old John hurried in.

"Lord have mercy upon us, what on earth are you doing on the floor?" he exclaimed.

"What in heaven, rather," said Alfred, scrambling up from his knees; but his servant was fussed.

"There was so much light showing under the door as I came along, I was afeared you'd fallen asleep, and the room was all afire. Well, I'm glad to find you still in one piece. Now look, here's a small helping of swan, and a nice little portion of carp; you will eat it, won't you, or our poor lads will be that disappointed."

Alfred did not tell anyone about his dream, but next morning he got up early as St. Cuthbert had told him, and he went out into the forest and blew his horn three times. And the birds flapped up out of the branches over his head, and the timid deer leapt to cover; but it was not the sound of the horn that alarmed them, it was the tramp, tramp, of five hundred armed men, coming to join their leader. These were the men of Somerset, Wiltshire, and Hampshire, who had not fled for fear of the pagans, but rejoiced to find Alfred alive.

So they camped in the forest of Athelney and rested there, polishing their weapons and swapping stories of atrocities. These were not exclusively Danish. There was a Viking skin nailed to the church door at Stogursey.

But Alfred disguised himself as a Danish scald or poet, and taking his harp he made the perilous journey to the enemy camp. And while he delighted the Danish warriors by singing their favourite war songs, his sharp eyes noted the casual watch they kept, and the weak points in their defences. So when he had seen all that needed to be seen, he slipped away by night, and made his way secretly back to Athelney.

Then he led his army to the causeway across Sedgemoor,

and up into the Polden hills. By the time dawn broke through the mist, the Danish camp was surrounded; before ever a dog barked, or a watchman shouted the alarm. God and the saints fought with the Christians that day, against the enemy host, and the slaughter was terrible; but when the sun dipped its bloody banners into the west it left Alfred victorious. Then he took pity on those who still lived, and received their hostages; while many he allowed to leave the kingdom immediately.

Crafty Guthrum was the chief of them all, and he announced that he wanted to become a Christian.

"But we can't have that disgusting Danish murderer *baptised!*" some of the knights protested.

"Baptism is the right of all who desire it," the king gently reminded them.

"Nasty heathen person," muttered his old servant. "No wonder *he* doesn't want to go back where he came from; they'd certainly hang him if he did!"

So Guthrum became a Christian, with many of his officers, and King Alfred was his godfather. The ceremony was at Aller, and a week later he was confirmed at Wedmore. In those days it was called Wetmoor, and it was an island; the sea around it was so deep that quite large ships could sail in. The remains of one were found early in the nineteenth century, when the moor was drained.

Alfred honoured Guthrum his godson, and his officers, and gave them many gifts, fine houses and land. But old John was right: Guthrum persisted in his heathen habits, and stayed an arrogant, crafty and bloodthirsty tyrant until he died.

But Alfred the Great, and Good, founded an abbey in thanks for peace, dedicated to Our Blessed Saviour and the Saints Peter and Paul. And many treasures have been dug up nearby, including a golden spearhead which may have belonged to King Alfred himself; while in 1693 the remarkable Jewel was discovered near Athelney, which is now in the Ashmolean Museum where it can still be seen. It has engraved upon it" – Aunt Mil cleared her throat – " 'Aelfred mec heht gewyrcan', which means, 'Alfred caused me to be made'."

"I've seen it," said Alice unexpectedly.

"What was it like?" asked Charlotte.

"Not terribly impressive, to me, because I was expecting something sparkly. But very interesting no doubt, if you know about old things," said Alice.

They had reached the main Bridgwater-Glastonbury road; Giles just made it into the stream of traffic. Alice drew in her breath in an audible hiss; but Aunt Mil sat erect and smiling with a well-bred disregard of danger. Most of the houses along the road had 'Bed and Breakfast' signs hanging by the gate. Glastonbury Tor rose on the right, as bald as a bell, topped with a ruined church.

"Now I can tell you something about that," said Giles. "The last Abbot of Glastonbury, whose name was Whiting, was hanged there when Henry VIII dissolved the monasteries in the sixteenth century."

"Did he pull down the church?" asked Vincent.

"No, I believe it was destroyed by an earthquake. It was another of St. Michael's. Where shall we have lunch?"

They found an empty field and sat there to eat their sandwiches. Charlotte stared at the smooth green sides of the Tor, like velvet from a distance.

"It's supposed to be hollow, isn't it," she said. "King Arthur's supposed to be sleeping inside with all his knights, ready to come out and fight for England in her hour of need."

"You'd think he'd've buzzed out for the Battle of Britain," said Vincent.

"That was aeroplanes, ass," said Charlotte witheringly. "King *Arthur* was a *knight*."

"Fat lot of use he's going to be then, when England has an hour of need!"

"Stop arguing, and don't hog the sandwiches," said Alice.

"It's the mound at South Cadbury that's meant to be hollow," said Aunt Mil. "Local people called it Arthur's Palace. A silver horseshoe was dug up there that was supposed to belong to Arthur; it was found in the track where he rides with his men on nights of the full moon. They ride round the hill, and then they stop to water their horses at the wishing well."

"Where's South Cadbury?" asked Charlotte.

"On the way to Wincanton, a few miles to the right. You can see it quite plainly from the road, a mumpy hill, a bit like the Tor," Giles told her.

"On rough winter nights people used to hear Arthur galloping with his hounds along the ancient track leading from Cadbury towards Glastonbury," said Aunt Mil. "There were supposed to be golden gates opening into the hill, and if you looked through them on St. John's Eve, you could see a king sitting inside, surrounded by his court. Then there are other stories about fairies. They used to steal corn out of the fields, but when bells were put into the church, the fairies went away, leaving their gold behind them."

Charlotte looked at Vincent, expecting him to scoff; but he was silent. Aunt Mil saw the look, however.

"Whether you believe all these stories or not, lots of people do, and always have," she said. "A party of antiquarians went to Cadbury, and while they were there an old man asked them if they had come to take the king away.

Cadbury Castle sometimes used to be called Camalat, as it is near a stream called the Cam; perhaps it is the same as the Camelot of the Arthur stories. As for *hearing* King Arthur: I myself know somebody who was looking at the ruins of Glastonbury Abbey, when she heard a noise of horses in the road alongside, a jingling and clattering like a troop of cavalry. So she rushed to the wall, and looked over; but there was nothing there; and she still believes that what she heard was Arthur and his knights."

"Have we got time to look at the ruins?" asked Charlotte at once.

"No," said Giles, getting up, and brushing off grass and crumbs. "We've got to get a move on, or we'll be late." He collected the picnic litter and buried it under the hedge, and when everybody had gone back through the gate, fastened it behind them. He hoped his children noticed his carefulness.

In a few minutes they passed all that is left of Glastonbury Abbey. Alice had been racking her brains since the picnic, and now said: "I thought they dug up King Arthur and Queen Guinevere – oh, ages ago; some time in the twelfth century?"

"Quite right," said Aunt Mil. "So they did." But Giles shook his head.

"Nonsense!" he said. "It was all a trick to get funds for the Abbey building. You can easily imagine how it happened. Announcement of divine inspiration to search for Arthur's body: screen of curtains to hide the monks who were digging: expectant crowd of faithful: hey presto!

King Arthur and his Queen have been discovered, admittance 10p., and buy your souvenirs here!"

"I don't see why you have to make a mock of it," said Aunt Mil. She sounded so hurt that he patted her knee.

"I'm not," he said, "but you have to admit that it was a put-up job. The monks had just finished the Lady Chapel and started on the main building, when the cash ran out with Henry the Second."

"Henry the Second – Fair Rosamund," said Charlotte.

"The same. Well, he died – in 1189 I think – and of course his son Richard the Lion Heart wasn't interested in Glastonbury: he wanted to fit out a Crusade and go and free Jerusalem. So suddenly there was no more money. Now in those days everybody knew about Arthur, his story was read and sung all over the country. So when his body was discovered in 1191 (note the timing) along with Guinevere's for good measure, everyone rushed to have a look, and donations flowed in. I reckon the divine inspiration was to *find* Arthur's body, not to search for it! It really was a stroke of genius, and the monk who thought of it deserved to be made Abbot!"

"But perhaps the bodies really were theirs," Alice objected.

"Almost certainly not. You see the real Arthur wasn't a king. We don't know much about him, but we do know that. But the lead cross marking the graves called him Rex – that was mistake number one. Mistake number two was even worse. The bodies – Arthur's and Guinevere's – were found lying in a hollowed oak, like a canoe. Now they were Christians; but does that sound like Christian burial?"

"He was taken to Avalon in a boat," said Alice, but she sounded doubtful.

"I am sure that it was Arthur and Guinevere the monks found," said Aunt Mil. "I am quite sure of it. Why should the holy men of Glastonbury put about a forgery?"

"But nobody thought anything of it in those days, Aunt Mil!" said Giles in exasperation. "It made life more interesting – it was a time of dragons and giants and fairies. You can understand it if you remember what the realities were – horrors like leprosy and the plague, and you might lose your wife and children and die yourself before you were thirty!"

Aunt Mil said no more, but she felt too cross to point out Fenny Castle on the left – not that there was much to see, it was just a queerly shaped mound covered in grass.

They had a wonderfully long view of Wells Cathedral – not a quivering arrow like Salisbury, that might at any moment shoot up into the sky, but a good old-fashioned parish church, well-settled on earth. Out of Wells they had to climb sharply into the Mendips for a mile or so. "All the people in this car seem to have eaten a lot of lunch," said Giles, changing gear. He glanced at Aunt Mil who usually enjoyed that kind of joke, but her face was stony.

The heavy trees along the top were curtseying in the wind. There was a statue among them on the right: twin babies suckling from a female wolf who was snarling round, on guard. "Romulus and Remus," said Giles, pointing it out and narrowly avoiding a motor cyclist.

"Who were they?" asked Charlotte.

"Founders of Rome. They were brought up by a wolf. This was originally a Roman road." And sure enough they could see miles of it in front of them, rising and falling like a switchback, straight as a throw.

"Did the Romans found Bath, Aunt Mil?" asked Alice ingratiatingly.

"Oh no – I think it's older than that," the old lady deigned to reply. Everyone waited expectantly, but more she would not divulge.

"I'll tell you how Bath was founded, if you like," said Giles. Charlotte and Alice expressing polite interest, he ignored Aunt Mil's silence, and Vincent's theatrical groan; and using his right hand freely to emphasise points in his story, he cleared his throat and began.

"There was great rejoicing when a son was born to King Lud-Hudibras and his lovely queen."

"What was she called?" asked Vincent.

"I am not at liberty to disclose. Shut up and listen.

After five daughters, it is no mean achievement to produce a son, and he was the apple of his parent's eye; they offered sacrifices of thanksgiving to the rising sun (as the custom was in those days), and hymns and prayers were chanted throughout the kingdom. His sisters spoilt him dreadfully: think of Charlotte with Harry, multiply it by five, and that is what they were like. The eldest was very good at embroidery, and worked him the most beautiful little suits. The second was an accomplished cook, and took charge of his kitchen, and baked him delicious meals. The third was clever at drawing, and his nursery was hung with lovely pictures of the birds, animals and flowers which abounded in the palace gardens. The fourth had a charming voice; she always sang him a lullaby when he went to sleep, and awoke him with music in the morning so that he should start the day in a good temper. And the fifth was his constant, dear companion.

His name was Bladud, and for fifteen years he was as happy as the day was long. Why not? He was handsome, strong and clever, and everyone loved and admired him. But alas, a wicked fairy must have slipped a curse into his cradle; or perhaps he unwittingly offended one of the spirits who inhabited the trees and streams around his home. At any rate, disaster struck.

He noticed one day that the skin on his hands was withering into grimy scales, and no matter how often he washed them, he couldn't wash them clean. This worried him a little, so he went to consult his youngest sister (they were all married by this time, but living nearby). Oh horror! as soon as he showed her his hands, she shrieked, and pushed him out of the house, and slammed the door on him! Poor Bladud turned pale as death, for now he knew what was the matter with him.

In those days people were frightened of dragons and wizards and demons and spells, of famine and pestilence and war. But among all these nightmares, real or fantastical, leprosy had a special, a terrible place. It was the lingering, deforming sickness, that divided a man from his friends. Every door, even his own, was shut against a leper; he was called unclean; he had to ring a bell to warn everyone to keep clear of him, for his companions could only be lepers like himself.

Bladud had taken it for granted that leprosy was something which happened to somebody else. He went back to the palace to find his parents. It no longer seemed like home. The familiar rooms seemed to shrink from him, as he passed through.

"My dear boy," said King Lud-Hudibras his father, "I hardly know what to suggest. What a frightful thing. You can't stay here, of course. If it was just a question of your mother and myself – but you see, there are the others to consider, your sisters, and our dear little grandsons; not to mention the Court. In my opinion, travel is the thing! A young man ought to travel, it broadens the mind. Take anything, my dear boy, that may be useful to you: furs, jewels, anything that might ease your lot. I should go at once, lingering farewells are so painful. No, if you'll forgive me, I won't embrace you – I have a slight cold." And waving his hand the king hurried away into the garden, where he inhaled deep breaths of disinfecting country air. "Take anything!" he called back over his shoulder. In fact he was very sorry for Bladud; but there was nothing else he could do.

The poor queen burst into tears. She kissed her son many times, and taking off one of her rings, gave it to him. "Wear this always," she said. "Never lose it. If you are ever cured, come back; no matter how you have changed, the ring will prove who you are."

So Bladud left the palace where he had lived so happily all his life. He had the clothes he stood up in, a hunting knife in his pocket, and a handful of precious stones which he took from the bowl on the table as he passed through the banqueting hall. But he left his horse and his dog behind; he was afraid they might catch the disease.

Well, it wasn't raining, that was something to be thankful for; and it was spring. By the time the bad weather came, he would be used to living rough. He trudged along the track through the forest. A startled buck leapt up almost under his feet, and sprang away through the trees. That evening he bathed in a clear brown stream, his supper was a clutch of bird's eggs, and snuggling into a heap of dry leaves, he slept soundly under the stars.

On the second day he couldn't walk so far because his feet were sore, but he made some useful discoveries. The silence had already begun to sharpen his ears, and when a bear came near he was able to avoid it. He had all the time in the world, so cutting down a couple of stout branches, he made himself a spear and a dagger, patiently peeling and chipping away with his knife, sitting cross-legged under a beech tree where the sunlight dappled the forest floor. He experimented with plants and roots, to find out which ones were good to eat. To spear a fish for supper gave him great satisfaction, and it smelt as good when it was grilling, as any palace banquet.

By the end of that day he had decided not to join a leper colony. The thought of being hemmed in by his own disease was too horrible; and he threw away the jewels he had taken from the palace. Since he was condemned to a solitary life, it did not seem that they would be useful for anything.

Every morning he remembered to say the prayers he had learnt at his mother's knee. And every night he made a notch on the haft of his spear, so that he would know how long it was since he left home. On the day of the seventh notch, the forest began to thin; he was already enough of a wild boy to feel alarm at this. Soon he was peering between the trees at a grassy shoulder of the down; and there, for the first time in a week, he saw another human being: a shepherd lying at his ease in a sunny patch, playing a curious tune on a little reed pipe, while his flock grazed peacefully round him.

The prince watched him from the bushes like an animal. The sight of a man reminded him that his hair wanted combing; and his voice felt so strange, he doubted whether words would come. However, at last he plucked up his courage and walked forward across the pasture. He felt very vulnerable, away from the trees. The shepherd put down his pipe as he approached, and watched him with a mixture of wariness and astonishment. It was true that a week in the forest had not done much for the royal clothes; Bladud's ermine suit was torn and stained, and one of the soles of his fur boots flapped when he walked. The shepherd feared he was one of the lunatics who it was said inhabited the forest. But the boy had a quiet dignity that was reassuring; and when the shepherd saw the tell-tale marks on his skin, his heart filled with sympathy for him.

"So, what's to do now?" he asked, when Bladud had told him his story.

"I shall have to spend the rest of my life in the forest, I suppose," said the prince with a sigh.

" 'Tis all very well in summer; but later in the year, when food is scarce, the wolves and bears will eat you. No, you must get within reach of human dwellings, or you'll not live to see another spring." The shepherd took up his pipe and played a tune while he considered. Bladud waited anxiously. The air was so still, he could hear the sheep cropping the turf on the down behind them.

"There's a farmer I know wants a swineherd," said the shepherd, after a while. "He's a funny old fellow, half-blind; you won't find him particular. You'd have your own quarters with the pigs, away from the house; it would be a roof over your head anyways. But p'raps you don't fancy such work."

"It's about all I'm fit for," said Bladud, looking ruefully down at his hands.

"Cheer up!" said the shepherd. " 'Tis a long road as has no turning, remember that, and every cloud has a silver lining."

"Won't your friend think it odd if I ask for work as a swineherd? My clothes – " Bladud blushed. "He'll think I'm a thief, I am afraid."

"You do look a bit of an odd fish, to be sure."

"I suppose I couldn't ask you – You wouldn't consider – "

"Swapping suits?" asked the shepherd, brightening. "Ho, yes! Why, the missus'll give them furs a wash and a scrub, and hang 'em out on the line, and they'll be good as new and make a whole string o'coats for the little 'uns! Ho, yes, I've no objection!"

So Bladud put on the shepherd's cloak and breeks, and very glad he was to get them. But looking at him, the shepherd was suddenly stricken.

"'Tisn't fair. Indeed your own mother would hardly know you!"

"She would," said Bladud, turning the ring on his finger. "If it seems unfair to you, though, give me your pipe as well; I'd sooner have that than anything in the world. It will keep me cheerful, when I am herding the swine."

"Willingly," said the shepherd, and he gave Bladud the little pipe made of reed; and then he told him how to find his friend who wanted a swineherd. They said good-bye, and Bladud walked off towards the village, which was called Keynsham, while the shepherd stayed with his sheep, and stroked the suit of ermines; he had never possessed anything so rich.

So Bladud was hired as a swineherd, and lived entirely with his pigs, even at night when they all bedded down together in a snug cave full of hay and dried leaves. And he thought he could have found worse companions. He kept them clean, so they didn't smell; they were polite and neat according to their nature, and couldn't complain, or spread slander. At dawn he led them into the forest, from glade to glade where the sun, slanting through the branches, lit golden pools between the trunks of the trees; or where the rain, whispering from leaf to leaf, hardly wetted the forest floor. Here he would sit and play the little pipe. When the greeny-gold treetops began to turn pink, and filled with the evening voices of the birds, the prince and his pigs returned to the cave, where the old farmer's wife had laid ready a meal of bread and cheese and milk. Only rarely did the people in the village catch a glimpse of him, and then they thought the farmer had done well to find such a hardworking young man for a swineherd.

So the weeks passed, and the months, and Bladud was not unhappy. But then disaster struck a second time. One morning he noticed to his horror that several of his pigs had hoary marks across their backs. They had caught his disease.

That night he did not dare to return to the farm; instead he took a narrow winding path, that led deeper and deeper into the forest. The pigs had grown attached to him, and followed him faithfully; sometimes he played a tune on his pipe to encourage them. When they had travelled together for several days, they crossed the river Avon, and now he thought he was safe."

"How did he get the pigs across the river?" interrupted Vincent. "They can't swim, they cut their throats with their forefeet if they do."

"He found a place where the river was wide and shallow," said Aunt Mil. "The little ones he carried in pairs, one under each arm."

"Exactly," said Giles. "And when they were all safely across, he built a strong shelter of branches well thatched with turf, guarded by a ditch and a double ring of stakes pointing outwards; and this became their new home. The pigs had individual stalls; he knew he couldn't cure their sickness, but he thought if he kept them separately, it might spread less rapidly.

Now one morning, while he was praying as usual to the rising sun, his sober pigs suddenly behaved as if they had taken leave of their senses. They lifted up their snouts and dashed away, squealing and bounding between the trees. Flashing a quick apology to the deity, Bladud snatched up his spear and ran after them; but they ignored his desperate cries: even the sick pigs were going like two-year-olds. At last they came to a great oozy bog, into which they rushed, and floundered about, plunging and wallowing with grunts and squeaks of pleasure. Bladud stood and watched them, and scratched his head, for they were enjoying themselves so much, he didn't know how he was going to get them back to their shelter that night. At last however he thought of collecting a quantity of acorns, which were their favourite food; and so he was able to tempt them home when the time came.

Now they had discovered the bog, it was no use trying to take them anywhere else, for they wouldn't go. And then Bladud noticed a very strange and wonderful thing. Their sore backs were beginning to heal. Evidently it did them good to wallow in the bog; and then it occurred to Bladud to try the same cure on himself.

So, day after day, for week after week, he joined the pigs in their mud bath; and at last his skin was as whole and clean again, as it had been when he was a child.

Then he collected a satchel of acorns, and with a last look round the shelter, he called to his pigs, and casting the acorns to guide them, he led them back across the ford, and through the forest. It was a perilous journey, for now the hard weather was coming and they could hear both bears and wolves too close for comfort; but the herd kept together with the little pigs in the centre, and Bladud guarded them with his spear and dagger by day, and with fire by night; and at last they reached Keynsham safely. And this time Bladud took his pigs down the main street with his head held high, playing a triumphant march on his pipe.

The old farmer was very indignant at first, but he had to admit that his pigs looked well, and had wonderfully increased since he saw them last. Then Bladud told him all that had happened. The farmer and his wife were astonished; and when they heard that they'd been employing a prince as a swineherd all this time, they both dropped on their knees in front of him and begged him to forgive them. But he soon put them at ease with kind and grateful words; and then he invited them to go back with him to the palace. So next day they set off, closely followed by the prince's favourite pig who would not be parted from him. They reached the palace on the Feast of Acorns, when it was the custom for the king and queen to dine in public.

Now Bladud had changed very much since he left home. He was taller and broader, and brown from living out of doors, and even his youngest sister didn't recognise him. So he took off the ring his mother had given him, and leaving his pet sow to make a way for him through the crowd, he leant over the queen's shoulder and dropped the ring into her cup of hippocras. When next she raised the cup to her lips she gave a great cry and sprang up from the table, staring wildly round. But Bladud caught her in his arms, and then she knew her dear son, perfectly cured, tall and strong and beautiful.

So Bladud gave the old farmer many rich presents, and hung a collar of precious stones around the neck of the faithful sow. And then he set out on his travels again. He went to Athens, where he studied for eleven years.

He returned full of wisdom, and when Lud-Hudibras died, and he became King, he founded the city of Bath on the site of the warm springs where he had been cured. It was called Carbren in those days. He built a temple to the goddess Minerva, and hospitals where the sick could stay while they were bathing and drinking the waters; as well as a splendid palace for himself, and fine houses for his nobility.

Do not suppose that he ever forgot the old farmer. He gave him an estate to retire to, near the city; in those days it was called Hogs' Norton, but the name has been changed to Norton Malreward. And in spite of the cares of state, he never neglected his studies. He became very interested in science and magic as he grew older, and they were the death of him at last. For in an attempt to fly, wearing wings he had designed himself and strapped to his shoulders, the optimistic old gentleman leapt from the temple of Apollo, and was dashed to pieces on the paving below.

King Bladud was succeeded by his son, King Lear. The place where he crossed the river with the pigs is still called Swineford."

"And if you look carefully," added the now entirely restored Aunt Mil, "you will see that some houses in Bath have ornamental acorns in his honour."

But there was no chance to look at anything before the concert. Alice and Charlotte had just time to find their seats in the Abbey and tumble into them, gasping, before the music began – music like flights of brilliant birds, that swept and circled and glittered, and soaring clung quivering to the vaulted nave.

Witches

The Hag is astride,
This night for to ride;
The Devil and she together;
Through thick and through thin,
Now out and then in,
Though ne'er so foul be the weather.

Robert Herrick

As summer drew into autumn, the weather broke, and it
rained most days. The stream below the house got back
its voice, and the woods their smell of leaves and moss;
the marks of wagon wheels leading down to the ford,
which had showed clearly in the heat wave, were hidden
by a fresh crop of grass.

John Sweeting, Giles' farm worker, was a middle-aged
man, shortish and stocky, with a way of standing with his
feet apart to tell you a yarn. He had beautiful eyes of a
limpid blue, and wiry black hair just flecked with silver. He
was related in some way to Mrs. Trim, and there was the
same feeling about him of simplicity and continuance. He
was like the soldier, the watchman, the gardener in Shake-
speare; and in painting, the man in the crowd who looks
on at a Nativity or Crucifixion, or wearing a crimson cloak
leads a horse in a Triumph: the extra, in fact, through
whom history is accomplished.

His father had worked at Pippenhay, and John himself

hadn't moved much with the times; he shook his head over Giles' ideas. But if something was discussed with him first, he usually finished by pointing out the value of it; and once Giles discovered this he felt more confident.

The fields at Pippenhay had names: Big Mead, Rising Veet, Bricklepark, Round Fall, Thirty Acres, Cribbus and Withy Beds. The covers had been planted by Giles' great-grandfather to shoot in; between the larches and oaks, dead trees hung. The hedges bulged between the fields, and all the ponds needed cleaning. Giles hired a man with a bulldozer to lay drains and dig ditches; he spent hours in the saddle room with John, poring over a map of the estate, planning where to dig to the best advantage, and what to sow in the autumn. This year he had sold his grazing; somebody else's heifers were gobbling Thirty Acres. Giles would buy his own in a month or two, and a bull to run with them.

Some of the farm buildings were as ancient as the house. There were swallows in one; the anxious parents swooped out whenever Giles darkened the doorway. Their nest was crammed with young, looking all beak from the ground because they had not yet grown their chestnut bibs. In another shed there was a wheel like an enormous capstan, that turned a mill for grinding apples. "Used to be worked by a horse," John Sweeting said. "Used to be a cider press alongside. Dad and Oaten and old Pat – they were young men then – they used to tighten up the press with a spanner. Eight feet long that spanner was; real hard work Dad called it!"

Old Pat still lived down the road. He had a small head, like a fowl's; his wattles were rosy with cider. He wore a battered hat in all weathers.

"Pity we can't get it going again," said Giles, laying his hand on the wheel. It still turned as if it had been oiled.

"Don't reckon 'twould make your fortune, Mr. Dory. You sell your apples to one of the big companies, that's your best bet. It's all that fizzy bottled stuff, that's what people want these days. Don't know what they see in it!"

Giles moved to the doorway. The archway opposite led into the old carriage house where the name of somebody's pony, Brownie, had been scratched above a stall. It was a very dark afternoon; as he watched, fat drops fell. The ivy wads on the buildings looked almost black. He switched on the light, and the low-powered, cobwebby bulb shed its circle of dusty gold between the wheel and the fertiliser bags and the table where he kept his keys. John Sweeting like an actor caught the light.

"Home-made cider could still be good business," said Giles. "I'm sure there'd be a market for it in London."

"Ah – London," said John, with a gentle movement of his hand that accepted its madness. "There's no knowing how they go on there."

A rumble of thunder shook the roof; the rain began to hiss. Giles turned back into the room.

"Like I see it," said John, taking his stand with his feet apart, squaring up to tackle the conversation, "you can't have it both ways. With costs like they are, you've got to make a profit. Take eggs. No-one who knows anything about anything would keep their own hens these days, with the cost of feed like it is."

Giles was silent. A dozen hens scratching round the back door was another of his dreams, and Aunt Mil had already offered to look after them; but he could see that she and a profit were incompatible.

"Don't think I'm one of the stick-in-the-muds who

want to live in the past," John went on. "It wasn't all golden then I don't expect; it can't have been. The good old days were the bad old days for some people."

"True," said Giles, seeing he was in for a lecture, and wondering how the new drains were running in Withy Beds.

"Supposing you needed a doctor – they had funny old cures for things. Or say your milk turned in weather like this, or the cow slipped her calf – you were out hunting witches immediately."

"Horrible!"

"Why, people would believe anything in those days! They were frightened I expect, and that made them cruel."

Giles wondered to himself whether people had changed as much as all that. A crack of thunder seemed to bounce off the roof. John Sweeting glanced upwards, shrugged, and spread out his hands.

"Now a clap of thunder like that was supposed to have carried off old Nancy Camel, and folks said 'twas the devil. Poor old woman! She'd 've been in an old people's bungalow today, on assistance."

"How long ago was Nancy Camel?"

"Now that I can't tell you, Mr. Dory, because I'm not acquainted with the fact; but it was when the women and girls used to work their fingers to the bone making stockings. She lived near Shepton Mallet – not in the village itself, but in the woods nearby. Her place was more like a cave than anything, and ill-natured people called her a witch. The young girls used to go and consult her, if they broke with their sweethearts; if a cow or a pig took sick, the farmer would shake his head and blame the old woman. She could cure the rickets and croup in children, but they were afraid of her; the boys hid in the bushes and threw stones as she went by.

She lived to a great age, and her temper and her rheumatics got worse every year. But still she worked day and night making stockings, though she was all bent and withered up, and as blind as a bat; and she was still the finest knitter in the village. So the other women began to say that she must have made a pact with the devil. He visited her, they said, and did her knitting for her; why, she even worked on Sundays, so that proved it! They grudged old Nancy Camel every penny of her earnings, and vowed no good would come to the gentry that bought her stockings.

It had been a terrible hot August, and not a dry heat, but a damp heat, if you know what I mean; low clouds that wouldn't break, and everything in that part of the country looking like it was gasping for a drink of water. Then the storm came. It was the worst thunderstorm even the old men could remember. The thunder crashed like the wrath of God, and the lightning was so bright, you could have read a book by it."

John paused for a moment. Around them, dramatically enough, the thunder ripped and tumbled, and the buildings across the yard were blotted out by the steaming rain.

"No-one had ever known such a storm, and as night came on, it got worse. And then, in the middle of it – " John Sweeting slightly raised his right hand – "a dreadful scream was heard! Just one scream, loud and piercing, that gradually was lost in the crashing of the elements.

But at last the tempest passed, and it was calm, clear morning. The village folks came out of their houses and looked round in dismay. There were trees torn up by the roots, and chimneys down. The river had burst its banks, there were animals drowned, and the corn left standing in the fields was a mess – driven right into the ground, it was, all smashed into the mud. The devil had been abroad, that was certain.

But then as people got talking, they remembered the terrible scream that had come when the tumult was at its height. Everyone had heard it. It had started on the stroke of midnight, and gone on ten minutes or more; and now some added to it, vowing they had heard the crack of a whip, and the creaking of wheels. Everyone agreed that the devil had come after his own; and the end of it was, that a party set off through the woods to find out how old Nancy Camel had weathered the storm.

You can imagine it was very wet and dark under the trees, with the water running off the leaves as if it was still raining. There was no screaming here; only the drip, drip of the branches.

They reached the place where old Nancy lived in a hole in the rocks. Her door stood open. A skein of wool lay draggled on the threshold nobody had ever dared to cross. One glance was enough: the cave was empty, the old woman had gone.

But her visitor had left his terrible mark behind him! The tracks of wheels, the imprints of hooves were graven there deep into the living rock, for everyone to see, and take warning by!"

"Poor old woman," said Giles. He had been quite lost in her story. "I suppose every time a child died or the crops failed, she was blamed. She must have been murdered, and her body hidden in the wood somewhere; they were all so superstitious, no-one would have looked for it."

"Ah, but that's just the point!" said John. "If they were

so superstitious, who would have had the nerve to do away with her? You can't answer that one! Some of these witches were really hated and feared, yet nobody dared to raise a finger against them. Besides, what about the marks outside her cave? Deep marks they were, deep in the stone. Well, they must have been made by something; stands to reason!"

"I expect they were always there, but nobody noticed them before. Or maybe the rock cracked in the storm; that's possible."

"'Twould hardly 've cracked in the marks of hooves and wheels, I don't believe," said John, shaking his head. "I haven't seen the rock myself, mind, so I can't tell; it was from my grand-dad I got the story."

"Well," said Giles, giving the mill wheel a push – it moved without a creak, having been better built than the devil's chariot, "they were brutal, ignorant times. She must have had a very miserable existence."

"Oh she did, for certain," John Sweeting readily agreed. "Those witches all did, I reckon, for all their devilment. Yet once you had that reputation, what was there to be done about it? You'd to get what you could out of the situation, and hope you wouldn't end up in the village pond, or a bonfire.

Now there was a man living near Bridgwater kept one or two animals for himself, a goat and a few hens; and he also had a large pig, who was the regular pet of the neighbourhood, for everybody brought him scraps, and he was so clever he would follow his owner about like a dog, and so tame he would eat out of his hand.

But one morning when the farmer went to his sty, and called him up as usual, the blessed animal wouldn't shift out of the straw. He was took so sick, he could hardly hold up his head; and you can imagine what a state the farmer was in. Fortunately there was what you call a white witch living in that neighbourhood, so off he went to him immediately, to tell him about his pig, and ask what he should do.

Well, he was told to go to the pigsty in perfect silence, carrying with him a piece of rough cloth, and two large pins. He had to lance each foot and both ears of the animal, and allow the blood to run into the cloth. Then he must take the two large pins and pierce the cloth in opposite directions; and then go back into his cottage and lock the door. Without saying a word to anyone he must place the bloody rag on the fire and heap some turf over it, and occupy himself by reading his Bible until the cloth was completely burned away.

The farmer followed these instructions with his lips pressed tight together in case any sound should come out of him; and so soon as the bloody cloth was burnt to ashes, he slapped down the Bible and hurried out to the sty. There was the pig on his feet again, stout and hearty, and wondering why he hadn't been fed that morning!

But the white witch had warned the farmer to expect an old woman, who according to him had bewitched the pig. And sure enough, an old crone did hobble up with a bucket of peelings, and asked after the health of the animal. The farmer did not answer her, or speak a word; only he took the bucket and chucked it with the peelings still in it into the ditch on her side of the road. Then he went to the sty and stood there with his back turned, until she went away.

Now about this time there was a lot of talk about a certain lane in Bridgwater, for every evening a white rabbit would be seen in it. It would run up and down several times – and then vanish into thin air! Boys tried to set their dogs on it, but that was useless, for it hadn't got the scent of an ordinary rabbit, and if a dog did run it too close it simply disappeared. Of course it wasn't long before the rumour went round that the white rabbit was really a witch. And this was where the farmer who owned the pig joined in. He lived opposite the old woman I've already mentioned, the one that brought him the peelings; and he noticed that every evening, just when the white rabbit was running about the town, a window in her cottage was standing open! Well, that clinched it! It was as sure as if he had actually seen her putting on a white fur coat and bounding off on four legs.

Then there was such a crop of miscarriages, and untimely deaths, throughout Bridgwater! There were such plagues of ants and earwigs and mice, such epidemics of measles and mumps, such fallings downstairs and boilings dry of pots; and it was all blamed on the unfortunate rabbit! So at last a gang of the boldest men decided that it must be killed, and they started to patrol the streets of Bridgwater; but still they couldn't catch it. They might creep up close enough for a snatch – and find themselves grabbing at thin air! But one night they trapped it in a garden which had a high brick wall all round it. There was only one way in, or out – a narrow passage between two cottages, what we call in these parts a dranget. So several of the party stayed on guard there, and the rest moved up the garden, as quietly as they could so as not to alarm the animal before they caught up with it.

Then our farmer himself spotted the rabbit, just the other side of some cabbages. He had only to reach out and grab it; but at the last minute he was suddenly scared. What if it turned him into a toad? What would become of his wife and family then, not to mention his pig?

However he didn't like to act the coward in front of his friends, so he made a snatch and got the rabbit by the ears. The rabbit was so surprised, it neither vanished nor turned him into a reptile; in fact it didn't even struggle as he carried it up the garden, holding it by the ears at arm's length.

But seeing it so docile, the farmer forgot how frightened he'd been; instead he remembered the danger his poor pig had been in, and what it had cost him to have it put right, and how it had screamed when he lanced its feet and ears. And all this made him so mad that he aimed a powerful kick at the rabbit, as he went along. So soon as he did this – the rabbit was out of his grasp. How he lost it, he never could tell – one minute he had it, the next it was off, streaking in front of him towards the dranget. The men waiting there saw it come, and tried to stop it, but it dodged between them, vanished, and was never seen again.

But as for the old woman who had caused all the trouble in the first place – she was laid up in bed for three days after, unable to walk about! And all because of the kick she got in her shape of a white rabbit!"

"And I suppose the devil came and collected her, next time there was a thunderstorm!" said Giles.

"Perhaps so; very likely!"

But at Pippenhay the storm was over; the wet yard gleamed and smoked, and the only sound was the chuckling drains. Indoors the electricity had paled, as it does on stage when the house lights go up: Giles switched it off.

"You haven't convinced me that those times were good to live in," he said. "I think I'll stick to the twentieth century, bottled cider and all!"

"Ah well," said John, heaving up a bundle of stakes that had been gathering dust in a corner. "Perhaps so. Now take this fencing: if we borrow the machine off Tom for driving them in, it'll save us breaking our backs doing it, like we used to in the old days! There's good and bad in all times. Don't ask me which is the better – blessed if I know!"

"So-Ho!"

For my part I'll run the hazard
of being thought any thing, rather
than a rash, inconsiderate man.

(Extract from a letter from the
Duke of Monmouth to a friend,
shortly before he invaded England.

When the gale came, it was easy to imagine that Pippenhay
was haunted. It ran up the staircase, it tumbled off the
roof, it knocked on doors and creaked in the panelling. It
shrieked through every hole and crack, chucked bricks
down the chimneys, blew up the curtains, and lifted the
threadbare carpets along the passages. At dawn it dwindled
to a banshee wail around the house; and then it died,
leaving a wreck of smashed slates and snapped-off boughs,
and all the runner beans flat in the kitchen garden.

The front door bell rang. Alice was busy with the baby,
Giles was out; Charlotte and Vincent raced to the door, and
reached and opened it together.

The visitor looked from one to the other of them. He
had a pink, out-of-doors sort of face that looked too young
for his white hair, though that fell over his forehead in a
boyish sort of way. His eyes were bright blue. He was
wearing a jersey, and old trousers tucked into gumboots.

"Mr. Dory about?"

"No, he's not," said Vincent. "I like your bike."

"Yes," said the stranger carelessly, glancing down at it, "I find it pretty useful." The motor bike was mostly black and orange, like a tiger, and looked as if it might spring away with him at any moment.

"Is it a telegram?" asked Charlotte nervously.

"Of course not, you date," said Vincent, walking slowly round the bike, admiring. "Telegram men don't have bikes like this."

"Ministry of Ag. and Fish.," said the stranger. "Spiller's the name. I suppose your father forgot I was coming."

"Sure to have," said Vincent. "That's Dad all over. I know where he is, though," he added, still eyeing the bike.

"He's down in Withy Beds," said Charlotte. "With the man who's doing the excavating. It's the field at the bottom."

"Shall I show you the way?" asked Vincent helpfully. "It wouldn't take us a minute, on that," he nodded at the motor bike.

"Sorry," said Mr. Spiller, swinging his leg over the saddle and propping up the bike and his crash helmet together. "Not unless your Dad says it's okay."

The three of them set off down the field, and splashed across the stream. In spring the opposite bank had bluebells and little blue irises, and enormous white chestnut trees. Now all was green and brown. They had to cross Thirty Acres; the heifers bunched up and trotted after them. Mr. Spiller took no notice of them, and Charlotte kept close to him, her heart beating fast. She was afraid of them, and ashamed, but she couldn't help it.

"What have you come to see Dad about?" asked Vincent.

"He wanted to talk about ditching. We know all about it in this part of the world. You've been across Sedgemoor, I daresay."

"Yes. It's got ditches between the fields instead of hedges; the gates look funny sticking up on their own."

"Sedgemoor where they grow withies for baskets. Where Alfred hid," said Charlotte.

"That's right. Where the battle was."

"What battle?" the children asked together.

"Why, the battle of Sedgemoor, 1685, the Duke of Monmouth's battle. King Charles the Second's bastard."

They reached the gate of Withybeds, but neither Giles nor anyone else was there. Only the excavating machine, like an immense yellow grasshopper, stood abandoned by a heap of freshly clawed mud.

"Will Mr. Dory be along soon, do you think?" asked Mr. Spiller.

"I should think so," said Charlotte. "I know he was going to work here this morning; he'll have gone back to the farm for something, I expect, or perhaps he's talking to John Sweeting."

"Go on about the battle," said Vincent.

"You ought to spend the night of July the fifth in the tower of Weston Zoyland church," said Mr. Spiller. "They say if you do, you can still hear the fighting. Behind the village there's a track leading to the battlefield. It's a sad sort of place. There's quite a few houses round about, yet it feels like a little desert. There's some old stone mushrooms there – you know, what they used to stand barns on, to keep the damp and rats out; and some old trees. It's very flat country. They say the Duke of Monmouth climbed the tower of Bridgwater church, that's several miles away across the moor, to spy out the land before the battle.''

"Who was fighting who?'' asked Vincent.

"Charles II was dead, and the Duke was fighting his uncle James II. The reason for it was partly religious, because the king was a Roman Catholic, while the Duke was a Protestant. Round here a lot of people supported the Duke. He'd already visited these parts and cured a Crewkerne girl of the King's Evil – that was a sort of eczema, and only the touch of a king could cure it. So the country people believed in him, and thought he ought to be on the throne. After the battle, King James sent down Judge Jeffreys – ''

"I've heard of *him*,'' Charlotte and Vincent said together. Charlotte went on: "We had a meal at the Tudor Tavern in Taunton. It was Judge Jeffreys' Court House.''

"No,'' said Mr. Spiller. "The court was held in the great hall of the Castle – that's where the Taunton Museum is now. Everyone hated Jeffreys; and then there was Kirke, have you heard of him?''

"No.''

"He'd been Governor at Tangier. Kirke's Lambs, his soldiers were called, because they had a lamb on their banner, and they were the most brutal men that ever were seen. They were quartered in Taunton, by the river – Tangier Wharf, it's called now; you can see it today.

One of Kirke's Lambs broke into the house of some people called Bridges. He was raging like a wild beast after the women, who had all gathered in the parlour for fear of the roaring of the guns. He came crashing in and attacked the lady of the house; but while the poor woman was struggling, her daughter Mary, who was only twelve, seized his sword and stabbed him to the heart, so that he fell dead at her mother's feet. Well, little Mary was taken to Colonel Kirke, and tried by a court martial; but I'm glad to say she was acquitted. Not only that, but Colonel Kirke presented her with the sword, and told her to be sure that it was passed on to the future Mary Bridges of her family."

"Not so brutal as all that!" said Charlotte.

"Ah, but that Kirke was really more of a beast than a man. One poor young girl came to plead for her brother's life, and the Colonel said he would release the boy, if she would spend the night with himself. So very reluctantly she agreed to the bargain. Next morning the brute told her to draw back the curtains, and there was her brother's body hanging from the inn sign!"

"What else did he do?" asked Vincent.

"He and Jeffreys between them squeezed blood and tears out of the West country. There was one poor old woman condemned to be burnt, just for giving shelter to two fugitives from the battle. There were so many killed in the fighting, not to mention the prisoners they hanged in chains afterwards, that the bodies were thrown all together into pits, and covered with sand. All those innocent people murdered – for lots of them had only a staff or a pitchfork to fight with: it was a bitter thing for the Duke of Monmouth to have on his conscience!

They say he slept at Catcott before the battle, in an old house in the churchyard field. For years afterwards people used to see a man walking about there at night, without a head, and everyone believed it was the unhappy Duke."

"Why didn't he have a head?" asked Vincent.

"Because his uncle James cut it off.

He's been seen within living memory for that matter, galloping hell for leather down a road near the battlefield, with his cloak flying, and his plumed hat pulled well down. No rest for him.

He was a good soldier, but he wasn't much of a commander. He rode out of the battle before it was over; he knew he'd lost, and he deserted his army. He was caught hiding in a ditch on his way to the coast. All the country was out looking for him, and somebody noticed his George glinting in the bracken."

"What was his George?" asked Charlotte.

"The Order of the Garter: it has a figure of St. George on horseback, killing the dragon."

"You'd think he'd've taken it off, if he was running away," said Vincent.

"He can't have had a lot of sense," Mr. Spiller agreed.

"He was a coward," said Vincent sternly.

"Think how horrible it must have been, though, with everyone after your blood! Dreadful! Like being a pheasant," said Charlotte.

"He died bravely," said Mr. Spiller.

A light rain began to fall. There were blackberries in the bushes by the gate, but the hazelnuts in High Sticks cover were not ripe yet. The trees were starting to turn in the woods on the hill, the different greens were touched with rust. The clouds were high, and moving quickly in the prevailing south-westerly; it wouldn't rain heavily today.

"The password given to the rebel army on the night of the battle was 'So-ho'," said Mr. Spiller. "The Duke had a London house in Soho Square; but the word also has a sporting meaning, 'So-ho!' is what you shout if you spot a hare. Long, long afterwards, local children used to play a game of King James' men against King Monmouth's men, and 'So-ho!' was the war cry of King Monmouth's men.

After the battle the prisoners were kept for a night in Western Zoyland church. One of them was a bit of an athlete, with a reputation for his long jump; and he asked the soldiers if they would let him jump just once more for his family to remember, before they hanged him. So everyone gathered to watch, and the soldiers unbound him, and he took a run and a jump, right across the rhine – that's what the ditches are called, down on the moor – and while they were still gawping with astonishment, off he went running for his life; and though they fired after him, he got clean away!

But have you heard the story of the Twins Mallet?"

"No," said Charlotte and Vincent together.

Mr. Spiller rested his foot on the bottom bar of the gate, and his folded arms on the top of it; and fixed his blue gaze on the line of the Blackdown hills.

"The twins were the sons of a blacksmith called Mallet, whose forge used to stand at the crossroads to Somerton, Taunton and Glastonbury. It was a good place for a forge, for such horses as didn't lose their shoes in the mud across the moor, would more than likely cast them on the rough hilly roads between the towns, so he stood to gain both ways. Besides he kept some of the best cider in the West country, so he always had plenty of customers.

Mallet lost his wife when she gave birth to the twins, but they grew into strong handsome men. John and Jack, they were called, and they were so much alike that in all the world only two people could tell them apart: their father, and the daughter of the miller at Walton Mill. Her name was Bina, and she loved them both as passionately as they loved her.

Old Mallet made no secret of the fact that he preferred John, the elder of the twins. He blamed Jack for having caused his mother's death, and he never forgave him. Naturally enough John grew up spoiled and headstrong, but Jack was very fond of him; and when they both fell in love with the same girl, he took it for granted that he would have to stand down, out of John's way. So he made excuses not to go to the mill, and if Bina came to the forge he was sure to be busy. Until then she really didn't know which of the boys she loved best; but when she saw that Jack was what she called backing out, she thought that John was more manly, so he became her favourite.

Now this was the time of the Monmouth Rising, and everyone that passed the forge had his own version of what was happening. As for old Mallet, he expected the Duke to march on London and wipe out the Government; but there were gloomy tales that he'd failed to take Bristol. It was hard to find out the truth of it, but one thing was certain: young John Mallet wanted to get into the fight, and he spent his evenings up at the inn on the hill, where plans were being made to join King Monmouth. His father encouraged him, and they both of them jeered at poor Jack, mocking him because he said he didn't understand politics, and calling him a coward.

The end of it was that John went off to join the Duke's army at Bridgwater. He went with high hopes, and loud talk of making his fortune. That night he crept across the misty moor with all the other poor country boys. He saw his hero, the Duke, gallop off in the middle of the battle; and as dawn was breaking he scrambled through some reeds and hid himself in a peaty ditch. All round him there were shouts and cries as the wretched prisoners were rounded up and loaded with chains, while he lay in his hiding place trembling from head to foot, expecting every moment to be discovered.

Back at the forge his father was waiting anxiously for news, and that was not long in coming. The battle was lost. Then old Mallet was at his wits' end worrying about what had happened to his beloved John. He longed to shut up shop and go out searching for him himself, but he did not dare to; everyone knew he favoured the Duke and it would look too suspicious. So he ordered Jack to go, and told him not to come back without news of his brother. And when he found John, he was to warn him not to return to the forge, but to go straight to the mill and ask Bina to hide him. The miller had always loudly despised the Duke and his followers, so no-one would think of looking for him there; while Bina loved him so much, she would be sure to take him in.

Off Jack went to find his twin – but cautiously, for any young man found wandering about was certain to be arrested. He was sick at heart, for he feared that if Bina was caught helping John, it would go hard with her. He knew the moor like the back of his hand, and he remembered a place where the reeds grew thick, where a highwayman had laid up for weeks before he was discovered; he guessed John might be there. Sure enough, as he crept close he heard a plover's cry, which had always been their signal.

He was just stooping down to give their father's message, when somebody shouted: "There's another of 'em!"

John ducked under the slimy water lying at the bottom of the rhine; but Jack had no time to hide. A party of soldiers grabbed him before he could run, and they hauled him away in spite of his shouts that he was innocent. Meanwhile John lay quaking in the slime, telling himself that Jack would get off – nobody would ever believe good old Jack was guilty.

But they did believe it. People that knew the twins, vowed Jack was John, and a regular firebrand, who always swore he would lay down his life for the Duke.

Jack begged them to send to his father, and ask him if he hadn't been at the forge all night, and sent out on an errand in the morning. So a soldier went to see the smith. But Mallet was frightened: first on his own account, because it was known he supported the Rising; second that if the soldiers realised they had got the wrong man, they would go on hunting for John. So he declared that he hadn't seen either of the twins for two days, and he had never sent Jack on an errand across the moor.

"You wanted to lay down your life for the Duke, did you?" roared the captain, when he heard what old Mallet said. "So you shall!" And poor Jack had to pay for his brother's folly. He was hanged on the battlefield.

As it grew dark the dreadful noises faded, and night came quietly on. Then John dragged himself out of the rhine, more dead than alive. He had only one place he could go to – the mill where Bina lived; and sometimes crawling, sometimes running when the panic was on him, he made his way there. Every bush, every post he passed, he thought was a soldier; his head was bursting with the hiss of the bullets; the dreadful clinking of the chains where the condemned men hung; the cries of women for their husbands, sons and lovers; and worst of all, Jack's desperate voice repeating, again and again: "I had nothing to do with it, I tell you! I had nothing to do with it!"

Bina was expecting John, and when he saw him creeping up the shadowy bank of the stream, she was half-mad with joy. She hid him in the loft over the mill, and he slept: so deeply that the corn grinding did not wake him, nor the sun at midday; it was the moon that roused him at last, striking its cold white arrow into his heart.

Bina came then. People had told her that John had been hanged. She guessed what had happened, and she was furious.

He thought she was going to hit him; he began to creep round the edge of the loft while he struggled into his coat. "Keep your voice down," he whispered, "your father'll hear – "

"Still scared!" she jeered. "Go on, run! I hope you swing! Clear off, before I fetch the soldiers! Run! Run! Your brother's on your back, John – you'll never shake *him* off!"

John scrambled down the ladder and ran; and Bina laying down her head on a sack of corn, wept, and wished she could weep her life away.

No-one ever heard what happened to John; he was never seen again in those parts. His father died a bitter old man. As for Bina, she never married. She said she hated men, but there was one she had loved, and still mourned in her heart – poor Jack, who died on the hanging tree."

"Girls are so thick," said Vincent. "She was going to make a mess of it anyway; if Jack hadn't died, she'd've married John. Have a blackberry," he said to Charlotte, not unkindly, offering a squashed purple handful.

"Here comes your Dad," said Mr. Spiller, looking back up the field, and sure enough there was Giles, walking towards them with the man who worked the excavator. A long conversation on ditching followed, with Vincent tagging along; but Charlotte did not dare to go back on her own through the heifers, so she went into High Sticks cover and sat on a laurel bough, until everyone returned to the house.

Then – oh joy! – Mr. Spiller roared up and down the drive three times with Vincent riding pillion, before he roared away.

King Ina

When all the world is young, lad,
And all the trees are green;
And every goose a swan, lad,
And every lass a queen . . .

Charles Kingsley

Aunt Mil had many old friends in the village – old in both senses of the word; and when she had nothing special to do in the house or garden, she jammed on one of her bowl hats, and went visiting. It wasn't long before Giles and Alice were involved: there was usually a prescription, or cobbled shoes or cleaning to collect when they went to Taunton, for none of these things could be done in the village. In return they were given presents, jars of pickled onions, or jam with a sugary crust, a cabbage, or a paper bag of runner beans. Charlotte had a bonnet knitted by one of Aunt Mil's friends. It was in red, blue and purple stripes, and made her feel rather self-conscious, but she sometimes wore it in the garden to please her aunt.

One Saturday, late in October, Aunt Mil had to stay indoors with what Mrs. Trim called 'a chesty cough'. Giles lit the fires in the smoking room, which could achieve a state of snugness more quickly than most of the other rooms if you added two oil stoves for background heating, and here she sat with a tray of tea and her tapestry. She was working new seat covers for the dining-room chairs, in coloured wools to match the curtains she was mending when she told Charlotte about the Duddlestones.

Charlotte had found some old-fashioned school stories in the library. She came in with one of them now, intending to have a lazy afternoon.

"What have you got there?" said Aunt Mil, peering over the canvas.

"It's 'Madcap Molly of Mowbray Manor'," Charlotte told her, thanking her stars that Vincent wasn't in the room.

Aunt Mil's eyes glowed. "Have you started it yet?"

"Yes, I've read a couple of chapters."

"Have you reached the place where the girls are having a midnight feast, and Daphne sneaks to matron?"

"Not yet." Charlotte couldn't help smiling at Aunt Mil's enthusiasm.

"Let me look."

Charlotte passed her the book. "Read it if you like," she said. "There are heaps more."

"Are you sure you don't mind?" Aunt Mil asked without raising her eyes from the page.

"Not a bit; go ahead."

The logs crackled cheerfully on their bed of white ash. The smoking room clock struck three. It was a clear, cold day; a gust of withered leaves rattled against the window.

Charlotte noticed a packet on the mantelpiece, marked 'MRS. HARRIS'. She picked it up.

"Is this for Mrs. Harris in the village, Aunt Mil? D'you want me to take it?"

"Oh my dear Charlotte!" exclaimed Aunt Mil, looking

up with a guilty start. "I clean forgot about it! Yes, it is for Mrs. Harris at Brock Holes – crochet cottons and I know she wants them particularly, for the sets she's making to sell at Christmas. I meant to ask you or Vincent to run down with them for me."

"Okay," said Charlotte. "I'll take them now. I don't mind," she said, and becoming embarrassed by her aunt's apologies and thanks, she left the room as soon as she could.

She went over the fields to the village. There was only a herd of dairy cows to negotiate, and she was up to that. The wooded hills had turned all shades of red and brown, and looked as if they were smouldering with spurts of flame; but the poplars along the farm drive were golden, and glinted in the sun and wind like money.

Brock Holes was an unmade lane, and a mud pie in winter. But it was a good place for early primroses, when the bulgy hedges were full of nests. Mrs. Harris's cottage had little windows like mean eyes. It stood in an orchard, where a few bright red apples still clung to the twisted trees – cider apples, they were, called Hellfire Jack.

There was no bell, or knocker. Charlotte rapped on the door and waited. She thought she heard stealthy movements inside; she had a feeling of being spied upon. Then Mrs. Harris's official door-opening shuffle approached, there was the grate of a bolt being pulled back, and the old lady appeared. Charlotte was immediately disconcerted by recognising one of her mother's skirts, a loud stripey affair, that Alice had recently given to a jumble sale. On top of this Mrs. Harris wore pink crochet round the body, with pale green knitted sleeves. Her bare legs were mottled pink and purple, like Victorian marble, and she had cut out the sides of her check felt slippers to make room for her bunions. Her head was egg-shaped, with her dark-brown hair in a thin plait over one shoulder, and her cheeks were tight and red as her own apples. Her eyes were black, and full of humour and intelligence.

Had Charlotte been an enemy, like the Welfare, or one of her sisters, she might have been caught by the emptying of a slop pail out of the upstairs window. But as a friend she was ushered indoors immediately, and the goods of the house were put at her disposal.

"Isn't that kind of your aunt," Mrs. Harris said, undoing the packet, and arranging the cottons on the mantelpiece, by the teacup her son had brought back from Hong Kong. It was made of the finest white china, and if you tipped it up to the light, you could make out a girl's face hidden under the glaze at the bottom. "I didn't think she'd forget, mind, not your Aunt Mil; she's a real friend to me, a real friend. Now you'll have a cup of tea, won't you; and perhaps as your bones are younger than mine, you wouldn't mind drawing me a little water from the well. Just fill up this jug for me, my dear, and that'll last me until tomorrow morning, when young Mrs. Sweeting always looks in after church."

The well was a hole in the back kitchen floor. The water had to be drawn up in a tin teapot attached to a length of string. It was some time before Charlotte got the knack of throwing down the teapot so that it filled with water, instead of floating on the surface. The tea was made by the time the jug was full, and she followed Mrs. Harris into the front room. There was Mrs. Harris's bed in a corner, covered with pieces of crochet. The chairs had crocheted antimacassars, and there were more mats on the table and the teatray. Apart from these works of art, everything in the room had an ill-assorted, rather grubby appearance, as if it had belonged not long ago to other people, and might soon move on somewhere else.

"And how are you settling in at Pippenhay?" asked Mrs. Harris, pouring tea. "And are you happy in our part of the world?"

"Yes – very," said Charlotte, struggling with both questions. "It seemed strange at first, after London, but now we all love it. No thanks, I don't take sugar."

"Oh, you must take sugar," said Mrs. Harris, putting two lumps into her cup. "It gives you energy. You can't do without sugar. Or biscuits. Have one."

"Thankyou," said Charlotte, feeling that it would be pointless to refuse, though she didn't much like currant biscuits – squashed flies, as they called them at home.

"It's strange settling into a new place, as I know," Mrs. Harris agreed. "You may think I've lived here all my life, but I haven't; I come from Somerton."

"Is that very far away?" asked Charlotte politely.

"About twenty miles. So you can imagine I felt very homesick to start with, for there weren't the buses then, and what with David on the way, I wasn't able to get home to see my mother. Well, you must go to Somerton; you must see the church. It has a beautiful ceiling carved all over with fruit and flowers; and if you look carefully you'll find a little barrel of cider tucked away up there. Is your tea all right?"

"Fine, thanks."

"I wondered why you weren't drinking it. Put some more sugar in, if you like; you need it after a walk on a day like this. It makes me shiver every time I hear the wind at the door," said Mrs. Harris, peering over her shoulder as if the house was surrounded. She took the poker and stirred the logs so that sparks flew up the chimney. "Apple," she said. "It burns up lovely. What were we talking about?"

"Somerton."

"That's right. One of the kings of England came from Somerton; did you know that?"

"No – which one?" asked Charlotte, gulping at her tea.

"King Ina."

"I've never heard of him."

"Never heard of King Ina?" exclaimed Mrs. Harris. She sounded so offended that Charlotte hastily added: "I'm not very good at history, I'm afraid."

"Nor am I, but I should have thought you'd have heard of King Ina! He lived hundreds and hundreds of years ago, in ancient Dark Age Britain. Think," said Mrs. Harris, with one hand raised for the drama of it, "of what it must have been like then. There'd have been a witch brewing up spells, and a saint praying for sinners in every village; and Giant Gorm's bones would still have looked like bones, where he fell on Brean Down."

"Is it terribly steep? I've never been there," said Charlotte.

"The Giant was fighting the Lord Vincent for the valley of the river Avon," Mrs. Harris told her severely, "and he was vanquished. That was what I meant when I said he fell. His skeleton has turned to stone now, of course.

In that faraway time, two kings divided the country between them, one ruling all the land north of the river Humber, and the other the south. He of the north had an only daughter called Adelburgh, who was beautiful and intelligent, but had an obstinate streak in her character. The king of the south was a good man, valiant and true, but he had no children, and this made his people anxious, as well as sorry when in the course of time he died.

A kingdom without a king is like a garden without a gardener, it soon goes to rack and ruin. Now all the wicked folk, the robbers and liars and murderers, who had hidden themselves in the good king's reign, came out into the open, and began to swindle and kill and thieve. It was no longer safe for honest men to go out alone after dark; instead folks put locks on their doors, and hammered bars across their windows.

Then the bishops and clergy of the realm gathered together in London, and said many prayers together when they begged Our Lord to instruct them, how they might discover a king who would rule them with strength and justice. It was then made known to them, that they should seek out a man whose name was Ina, and he would bring back the land into peace and prosperity.

At this there was great rejoicing, and heralds galloped off at once in all directions to spread the important news. Bands of heroes followed, all eager to find the future King Ina; for this was the golden age of the quest, and while the noblest among them sought honour and glory, the rest expected that the new king would be certain to reward his discoverers, which was more than could be said for unicorns, corkindrills, basilisks and the other fabulous beasts men hunted in those days.

However, the Quest Royal (as it was called) turned out to be unexpectedly complicated. For as soon as the news got about, a great many young men who fancied themselves as king pretended to be Ina, and this was very confusing. Then, the heroes had set out in spring, when the country was full of flowers and the woods were leafy, and it was no hardship to live out of doors: yet time dragged on, and still the real Ina was not to be found, while the corn was in, the last fruits had been eaten, and nights were getting chilly. So, one by one, the heroic bands gave in, not to the robbers and wild beasts who attacked them, but to the longing for clean dry clothes to put on, and something hot to eat, and a warm bed to sleep in.

A group of knights who had been searching for Ina in the west, were going back home very tired and dispirited, when they happened to pass through a settlement of the name of Somerton. They noticed a man ploughing there, and they were watching him in an idle sort of way as they rode along; when suddenly, to their astonishment and joy, they heard him shout: "Ina!" And then again he shouted: "Ina! Come bring thy father's oxen, lad, and finish the row!"

With one accord the knights leapt the little ditch dividing the field from the track, and converged upon the ploughman. "*Who* were you calling?" one of them demanded breathlessly, losing his syntax and one of his stirrups in the excitement of the moment.

The ploughman was rather taken aback by the charge of destriers, but he pointed across the field. The heroes stared as one man in that direction, and there presently came into sight a pair of oxen, driven by a handsome youth. As soon as they saw him they knew that he was the king they had travelled so far to find, and immediately leaping from their chargers, they swept off their plumed helms and knelt in the mud as he approached. The ploughman regarded them with astonishment. So did Ina; and when they explained what was in store for him, he simply stood there with his mouth open, like any country bumpkin.

By this time a small crowd had collected, and the matter was discussed at length. Ina was a favourite in the village, and everyone agreed that such a good young man shouldn't be allowed to go to such a wicked city as London. And the heroes could only persuade the simple people of Somerton to let him go with them, by giving a solemn pledge that no harm should come to him, and promising to bring him home safely, should he for some reason not be crowned king.

However, as soon as the chiefs and nobles of the realm saw Ina, they were delighted with him. No fault could be found with his open manners and handsome appearance, and he was made king there and then, and immediately consecrated by the bishops.

A little while after this, a strangely clad messenger arrived at the court, a man of such rough behaviour and outlandish speech that it was difficult for anyone civilised to understand him. He brought news from the north; it appeared that the ruler on the far side of the river had recently died, leaving as his heir his only child, the lovely Adelburgh. When King Ina heard this, he sent a royal embassy to the princess, bearing rich presents, and a proposal of marriage, with the intention that their two kingdoms should be united.

The lovely, but wayward Adelburgh was pleased with the presents, but scorned the proposals of marriage. She was, after all, very young, and the idea of marrying a farmer's boy did not appeal to her. So she sent another of her painted, kilted heralds to decline Ina's offer; but morning and evening she looked at herself in the beautiful little mirror he had sent her, while her maidens brushed her hair.

King Ina was not put off; he guessed the true reason

for her refusal, and decided to go and see for himself whether she was worth pursuing. So he took off his royal clothes and dressed himself in his own livery, and pretending to be one of his own messengers he journeyed north and came at last to Adelburgh's castle. She received him graciously, and he repeated the proposals that had been made to her before.

"Dear me!" she said. "Your king is very persistent. But I suppose I could hardly expect *him* to know that when a *lady* says no, she means it."

Poor Ina would have blushed, except that she was so beautiful, he was blushing already.

"Is he then mistaken in recalling that in 'The Language of Love', 'no' from a lady as often means 'yes'?" It was the best he could manage; he tried not to mumble, and finished off with a courtly bow.

"You are witty, sir," she said, and this time it was her turn to blush. She wondered if he could tell that she had never read 'The Language of Love'. Her only source of books was a small mobile library consisting of a monk on a donkey, and he carried nothing but religious works, and never made it to the castle in bad weather. She rose from her granite throne, her brilliant tartan robes shifting and glowing in a cacophony of colours. "Come, men – " she summoned her bodyguard, who had been lounging about the heather-strewn banqueting hall, picking their teeth and tuning their bagpipes and talking to the hounds – "the audience is over for today," and she swept into her private apartments.

At least she had not dismissed him, and the anxious king considered what he should do. He was so much in love with her, his personal feelings now far outweighed the advantage to the state; he simply couldn't bear the thought of returning to London without her. Besides, he suspected that she liked him; there was a telltale, half-ashamed spark in her eyes when she looked at him, that made him hope. So he decided to ask for permission to remain in her household, and sure enough, she readily agreed; and he changed his neat livery for the curious clothes her people wore. And every day he found an excuse to exchange at least a few words with her: and by and by he hoped – he believed that she began to look forward to these encounters; it seemed to him that her face lit up when she saw him there.

He found the winter very dreary in the north, and the castle very cold and inconvenient. They were snowed up for weeks on end. The practical jokes got on his nerves; he found it difficult to raise a laugh when somebody pulled his chair away as he was about to sit down, or put apple dumpling in his bed, or swapped his clothes with those of the smallest servant in the castle. He didn't understand the poems they sang or recited after dinner, heroic all of them, running to never less than thirty verses, and ending in bloody death. Then they were forever telling him about the ghosts that haunted the castle, and when they saw he wasn't frightened, they dressed in sheets and jumped out at him from dark corners. And he resented the fact that while they were always eager to borrow his money, they jeered at him for lending it. Worst of all was the skirling of the pipes; it set his teeth on edge.

But Adelburgh was like the sun, even on the dreariest days. She guessed when he was homesick, and asked many questions about the palace in the south. He gathered that she imagined everything was much grander there, and more civilised; but he didn't press the point. Instead he

worked in a compliment, something about "the brightest
star in the Northern Lights" that made the richest jewels
in the south pale by comparison; which gave him a
chance to observe how beautiful she looked when she
blushed.

When the snow melted into the miracle of spring, and
travelling was once more possible, a great feast was
planned for all the nobles in the kingdom. Several
hundred guests were expected, and King Ina had an
uncomfortable feeling that some of them would try to win
the love of the lovely Adelburgh. He had already been
asked to bring the dishes to the royal table, an honour
among servants, and a chance he could not afford to miss.
So on the evening of the banquet he dressed in his finest
clothes, which he had brought with him and kept carefully
packed away. He looked more gorgeous than any of the
noble guests at the feast, and poor Adelburgh, who had
been a little in love with him for a long time, lost the
rest of her heart that night.

So she rearranged her household, and offered him rooms
in her own part of the castle; and now she made excuses
to see him, and be alone with him, on all possible
occasions. But her heart was heavy, for she still believed
that the handsome young man was a servant, and
however proud and wayward she was, she knew she
couldn't marry him.

One beautiful morning in early summer they were
standing together in the park surrounding the castle, for
the princess was considering planting a rose garden,
simply in order to ask his advice about it. They were
discussing whether roses would thrive so far north, and
looking ardently at each other, when a wild boar moved
out of a thicket. Adelburgh was too frightened even to

scream, but with a swift movement King Ina drew the little dagger he always carried in his belt, and hurled it with unerring aim. The boar fell dead without a sound; but Adelburgh gave a cry as if he had stabbed her, for it was death for a commoner to kill any royal beast, and she knew all her bodyguard had seen it.

"Ah, my poor boy, you are dead – dead as the brute yonder!" she cried in anguish.

"Dead only if you turn away your face – then, dead indeed!" he told her passionately – he was more at home in courtly language by this time. "I am Ina – that unhappy king who loves you devotedly and for ever," and conscious that he had burnt his boats, he took her speedily in his arms.

"*You*, Ina?" she exclaimed in delighted astonishment, wholeheartedly returning his embrace.

By this time the bodyguard had run up with drawn swords, so Ina told them his story; while Adelburgh marvelled at his great love and constancy, and eagerly agreed that they should be married as soon as possible. It was suggested to the castle poet that he might compose something to mark the occasion; but he was an angry old man, and wouldn't write a ballad with a happy ending.

So King Ina returned to his own country, and made royal preparations for the wedding; and everything being ready, he sent a splendid embassy to conduct his lady to him. And when she arrived at Wells, which was called Cideston in those days, they were married with pomp and ceremony, and lived happily many years."

"That's a lovely story!" said Charlotte.

"I'm only surprised that you never heard it before! I suppose you went to a London school. You'd think they'd have taught you some history!"

Charlotte carried the teatray into the tiny kitchen and put it down by the sink, where a dirty little window peered into a patch of stinging nettles. Meanwhile Mrs. Harris had hobbled across to the bed, and was sorting through the pieces of crochet.

"I want to make your aunt a duchess set for Christmas," she said. "She's been so good to me. What colours do you think she'd like? I'm fond of the purples myself. Here's a pretty one."

She had worked the mats – one large and two small – through all shades of purple from a lurid pink at the centre.

"I should give her the ones you like," said Charlotte carefully. "I'm sure she'll be pleased."

"But you must be going on home, my dear," said Mrs. Harris. "I wouldn't like to think of you walking all that way in the dark. Here, take some sugar lumps – I always keep a few about me." She fumbled in her pocket and produced two, rather grimy. "Suck these on your way, you'll find they keep you going."

Charlotte thanked her, and set off. Mrs. Harris watched from her lighted doorway until she was out of sight.

Pounce liked sugar lumps, so he had a treat. Charlotte found another school story and settled down with Aunt Mil in the smoking room; but she fell asleep before the end of the first chapter, and dreamt strange dreams about the many-palaced Ina.

A Christmas Story

And singers too a merry throng
At early morn with simple skill
Yet imitate the angels song
And chant their Christmas ditty still

John Clare

It was the Christmas holidays. Alice and Mrs. Trim spent most of their time in the kitchen, mixing the cakes and mincemeat whose warm scent filled the house like incense, and sweetened the nostrils of the postman when he called with cards and parcels.

"Quite like old times!" trumpeted Aunt Jane, who had moved in for the season against Giles' better judgement. Alice had invited her because she couldn't bear to think of her spending Christmas alone; but as it turned out her visit was unexpectedly useful, for she occupied Aunt Mil, and stopped her from invading the kitchen to help with the cooking.

Aunt Mil was not a good cook. She had made one Christmas pudding, mostly of carrots and prunes, from a recipe she had discovered in wartime and still treasured for its economy; it had boiled dry and ruined a saucepan. Now she undertook to guard Aunt Jane, keep her away from anything breakable, and prevent her cigarette ends from setting the house on fire.

Giles took the tractor and trailer, with Charlotte and Vincent in it, down to High Sticks cover to look for a Christmas tree. There was a muddy pond in the depths of the wood, and they had to clamber through ivy and brambles, and over the mossy trunks of fallen trees. But at last Giles saw what he wanted: a fir that had had no chance to grow beyond a tuft of branches at the end of fifteen feet of trunk. So he hacked it down and cut off what they wanted, and the three of them hauled it through the wood to the trailer. Charlotte and Vincent climbed in and sat beside the tree, with their clothes full of bramble and the smell of pine in their noses, while Giles turned with a flourish and trundled them back across the fields.

All went well until they reached the ford. They got through it all right, but the further bank was a foot or so deep in mud, and here in its own ruts the tractor stuck. In the end Vincent had to run back to the farm and hunt out John Sweeting, and he borrowed another tractor from someone in the village, and a length of chain to haul them out.

Charlotte and Alice decorated the tree with ivy and fir cones, bunches of grapes from the old vine in the garden, and teasles from the hedge; these had been painted silver or gold, and they looked lovely. When it was all finished everyone sat round the fire and drank hot wine with sugar and lemon and cinnamon in it, and roasted chestnuts on a shovel. Aunt Jane drank as much wine as anyone, but she took the precaution of diluting it with the mineral waters her doctor had prescribed for her, and the combination must have been too much, because she fell asleep in her corner of the sofa, with her head tilted back on the cushions and her mouth open.

"Poor Jane," said Aunt Mil, with a pitying glance. "Her constitution is not, I fear, what it was."

"I don't know," said Giles. "If I drank gin mixed with cheap red wine, it would double me up for days!"

"Hush!" said Alice, glancing at the children. Charlotte was finishing a Christmas present for Mrs. Trim – an embroidered kettle holder – and didn't hear; but Vincent said loudly: "*I* didn't believe it was water, whatever she said! Whoever would carry *water* about in a *gin* bottle!"

"Poor Jane," repeated Aunt Mil, with a reproving shake of her head at Vincent. "Duplicity is not in her nature."

A chestnut burst, making them all jump.

"How are you getting on, Charlotte?" Alice asked kindly.

"All right, I suppose. She's bound to have one already, and she could have made it better herself, but I suppose it's all right."

"It's the thought that counts," said Aunt Mil.

Harry was lying in his carrycot, in his night clothes. He was quiet, but not asleep; he was staring at the scarlet shaded lamp. He had dear fat cheeks, like the babies who blow the winds on old maps. Charlotte had made him an owl of brightly coloured felts; it was the nicest of her presents.

"I wish they still had mummers," said Vincent, trying to pick out the scraps of chestnut that had wedged under his nails. "Will anybody come here carol singing, Aunt Mil?"

"I shall," said Charlotte. "I'm going out tomorrow with the church choir."

"I wish it would snow," said Vincent. "I wish we could go tobogganing on Christmas Day."

"It won't," said Giles, taking the red hot shovel off the fire, and tipping the chestnuts into the fender to cool. "John Sweeting says it hardly ever does before Twelfth Night."

Aunt Jane stirred, smiled, and moved her head into a more comfortable position without opening her eyes.

"Talking about carol singing," said Aunt Mil, "do you know the story of Nancy Hawkins?"

"No," they all said. Vincent made a dive at the chestnuts, and burnt his thumb. "Tell it," said Alice.

"Nancy Hawkins was an old widow woman, who lived in a poor little house in Street."

"Street near Glastonbury, where Clarks make shoes?" asked Charlotte.

"That's right; but in those days it was only a village.

Her house was in the meanest part; the lane where she lived was so narrow, that people living on opposite sides of it could shake hands without moving from their doorsteps.

The old woman was a cripple, and hardly ever went out, but stayed all day in a single room, which had a wide open hearth with an overhanging mantel, a couple of chairs, a dresser and a little round table. There were a few cups and dishes put out on the dresser, and one or two souvenirs on the shelf over the fire; but all in all there wasn't much to keep clean, and when her work was done Mrs. Hawkins used to sit by the hour on a settle against the hearth, gazing into the fire which she fed with peat, while a smoky black kettle hung over it from a hook.

She had had seven children, but four of them lay in the churchyard, though she had taken them to the wise woman who worked many cures. Of the three remaining, her daughter Susan was a maid in the squire's house at Shapwick, and her daughter Betsy was married. And then there was her best-loved, George.

After her husband died, she and George lived together for a while, and then he told her he wanted to go to sea. That was a blow; but she wasn't a woman to make a fuss, so she didn't say much about it. He said good-bye to her on the doorstep, and everyone in the lane turned out to wish him well, but kept a respectful distance.

"Now don't you worry about me, Mother," he said. "Don't expect to have a letter, for you mind what a labour I found it writing at a school desk, and I don't think I could make anything of it aboard ship! But I'll be back in a year, with the spring; I promise you that." Then he kissed her, and took up his bundle, and went off waving and smiling to the neighbours; and Nancy watched till he was out of sight, and then she turned and hobbled inside, and shut her cottage door.

It wasn't so bad in the summer, when the sea and the sky were calm and blue. But in autumn the gales came, tearing the leaves from the trees, driving the white horses at a gallop up the Bristol Channel; and she trembled to think what it must be like in the ocean. She lay awake night-times listening to the wind, hardly hoping her George could be still alive. And she had no means of getting news of him, she didn't even know the name of his ship.

And then it was spring. There were lambs and primroses and pussy willows, and birds so busy with nesting that they almost flew into you; and young George Hawkins walked up the lane and in at his mother's door. He had to stoop to get inside, for he had grown inches; he was strong and brown, and he had a bag of curiosities to show, and stories just as strange to tell.

All the neighbours crowded up to greet him, and the treasures were passed from hand to hand – the shell as round as a ball, with stripes and spikes, that he had bought in Vigo; the pickled mermaid's tail from the Azores; the dried baby from Manaus on the Amazon. Most of the spikes had rubbed off the shell, and the stripes had faded, but it lit up beautifully if you held it over a candle. Somebody suggested burying the baby, but as George pointed out, it wasn't a Christian. Nancy reckoned it looked more like a monkey; and as for the tail, you could find one any day in the fish market, called cod. George explained that it had shrunk and faded in the pickling; its original colour had been a wonderful shade of pink.

When George started yarning, they all scratched their heads. Whoever heard of fish that flew? or waterspouts as tall as the church tower? or balls of fire that flared on the mast without burning it?

Young George stayed until his money was spent, and his tales all told, and then he was off again. Old Mrs. Hawkins put the shell on the mantelpiece, and she wrapped the baby in a paper bag and laid it in the dresser drawer; but she kept the mermaid's tail outside in a bucket of salt water, because it had started to smell. Winter came, and icy winds screamed between the houses, rattling the slates and knocking off chimney pots; but Nancy comforted herself with the thought that George's captain must be the best in all the world to steer safely through so many dangers.

And the next time George came home, he brought lengths of silk for his mother and Betsy and Susan, silks far finer than anything the squire's wife wore. He stayed several weeks, and old Mrs. Hawkins began to think he might settle down at last; but no, there was no girl pretty enough to keep young George from the sea.

So he went away again, and she waved him out of sight with a cheerful heart.

It was a very cold winter. The flat wet country round Street had a skin of ice, and the willow trees were all cased in glass. The bell-shaped tor was white with frost, which lasted all day without any sun to melt it. The smoke from the village chimneys flowed straight up into the sky, and the icebound world seemed frozen into silence, for the children had to be kept in in such weather. You could hardly tell when night turned into day, but for the morning mist like dying breath gasped out under the glassy trees.

A few nights before Christmas, Nancy Hawkins was sitting over her fire as usual. She was thinking of her family: her dead husband, and the little ones round him in the churchyard, and of Susy and Betsy who would be along to see her in a day or two; but mostly she thought of George. She got great pleasure from imagining his voyages, even if she didn't believe everything he told her when he came home.

She was thinking and dozing and thinking on, when she became aware of a marvellous singing. It was so faint at first, she only caught snatches of it; but gradually it came closer. It was the carol singers for certain: Betsy's little boy was in the choir, and she guessed he had persuaded the others to come and sing for a surprise for his granny. She got up, and felt along the mantelpiece for the jar of peppermint lumps she kept for children.

But it was the most wonderful singing, more beautiful than anything she had ever heard. It filled her with peace and joy. She forgot about the sweets. She lost all sense of time. It was as if the soul in her crippled old body had woken up, and was stretching its wings.

The singing stopped, and she came to herself. She expected a scuffle outside, she waited for the door to open, and a cheerful voice to call: "Merry Christmas, Mrs. Hawkins!" She was ready to answer: "Well, come in then, one of you; I suppose I'd better give you a few sweets for your trouble."

But nothing happened. So she hobbled across the room, and opened the door, and looked out. The passage between the houses was empty. She stared about. Snow had fallen; the last flakes were still floating down. But there were no footmarks between the houses; no marks at all.

The woman who lived opposite opened her window and cried: "You all right, Mrs. Hawkins?"

"Did you hear that singing just now?"

"What singing, my dear?"

Mrs. Hawkins didn't answer. The woman waited a moment, then called: "Good-night, then!" and shut her window and the curtains. Mrs. Hawkins threw an apron over her head and hobbled as fast as she could to the end of the lane. Not a soul – to right and left the road was quite empty.

Then she came all over atremble, and crept back into her house, and sitting down by the fire she began to weep. For it had come into her heart that her George was dead; she was certain of it; she would never see him alive again. And the singing she had heard was angel voices, welcoming him into his glory."

Aunt Mil paused. Giles softly put another log on the fire. Nobody felt like talking. After a minute or two, Aunt Mil finished the story.

"Sure enough, some long time after, a letter came for old Nancy from George's captain. The boy had died, that night before Christmas. One of his mates had been swept overboard in a high sea, and George had tried to save him, and been drowned.

So he laid down his life for his friend; but Nancy believed that his last thought was for his mother, and that God allowed him to send comfort to her with the heavenly music. And it was said that just before she herself died, very aged and bedridden, the same wonderful singing filled her poor cottage."

They sat on a while by the fire. The chestnuts were eaten. Little Harry had gone to sleep.

Outside the ground was iron hard; the river's brink had a frill of ice; the hedges and trees, picked out with a sparkling pencil, glittered under the moon. One leaf fell from the kestrel oak, in a slow spiral, with a papery sound. The dog fox slipped out of High Sticks cover, through a stiff fringe of grass that brushed his fur with frost. A little owl glided like a thought or a dream into the trees near the house; the moon eyed its own round face in a windowpane.

Downstairs, Giles looked between the curtains for a moment before he turned off the light. "It's pretty cold after all," he said. "Vincent may get his snow."

The books containing these legends and old wives' tales could all be found in the library at Pippenhay. A Victorian lady, Mrs. E. Boger, published in 1887 a stout volume called 'Myths, Scenes & Worthies of Somerset', in which she wrote at length about the Duddlestones, Fair Rosamund, and King Bladud of Bath. Another Victorian, Mr. C. H. Poole, had still more to say about Bladud, as well as describing King Ina's courtship. He put in the tales about Nancy Camel and the Bridgwater Rabbit Witch, the Midsummer Eve Vigil and the Dancers of Stanton Drew. He gave a not entirely accurate account of S. Wulfric, and quoted the story about the Fairies from a very much older book, 'The Pandemonium, or, The Devil's Cloyster', by the Rev. Bovet (1684).

One of Aunt Mil's favourite books was by Miss Frances Hariott Wood. It was full of homely country stories, including the tragedies of Tom Cox and the Twins

Mallet, and Nancy Hawkins' Christmas. It was called 'Somerset Memories & Traditions' (1924).

There were many books about King Arthur and King Alfred, ranging from Geoffry of Monmouth's inventions to 'Arthur of Britain' by E. K. Chambers. Aunt Mil had read and believed them all bar one. This was a new addition to the library; it belonged to Giles, and was called 'The Glastonbury Legends' by Professor R. F. Treharne. It was full of fascinating information – for instance, that there were pelicans and beavers on the Glastonbury marshes two thousand years ago; but it also spelt out the argument against the Glastonbury Graves which Aunt Mil found so distasteful.

Then there was a 'Calendar of Customs, Superstitions, Weather-Lore, Popular Sayings & Important Events', reprinted from the Somerset County Herald in 1920, that brought back life in Somerset as it used to be.

Photoset and printed in Great Britain by
Lowe & Brydone Printers Limited, Thetford, Norfolk